WEIGHT TRAINING FOR SPORT

Bill Tancred and Geoff Tancred

With a foreword by Ronald J Pickering

HODDER AND STOUGHTON
LONDON SYDNEY AUCKLAND TORONTO

British Library Cataloguing in Publication Data

Tancred, Bill
   Weight training for sport.
   1. Weight lifting
   I. Title   II. Tancred, Geoff
   796.4′1   GV546.5

ISBN 0 340 34449 0

First published 1984

Copyright © 1984 Bill Tancred and Geoff Tancred

Third impression 1986

Printed and bound in Great Britain for
Hodder and Stoughton Educational,
a division of Hodder and Stoughton Ltd,
Mill Road, Dunton Green, Sevenoaks, Kent
by J. W. Arrowsmith Ltd, Bristol BS3 2NT

Phototypeset in 11/12pt Century Schoolbook
by Rowland Phototypesetting, Bury St. Edmunds, Suffolk

Contents

Figures

Tables

Foreword

It seemed to me that there were at least two good reasons why I should try to squeeze some time in the midst of a very hectic life to write a foreword to this book, *Weight Training for Sport*.

The first really is an excuse to make public a long-felt tribute to the remarkable athleticism of the whole Tancred family. Adrian Tancred, himself a very talented all round sportsman, was indeed fortunate in choosing as a wife Elsie who not only matched his enthusiasm for sport but managed to produce three boys, all fine physical specimens. Geoff, one of the co-authors of this book and by far the smallest of the trio, had to settle for being a good hammer thrower at County and AAA's level. Bill, the other co-author, was a very athletic giant who might still lay claims to being the best all round thrower ever in British athletics; and not far behind him in that race would be another brother, Peter, who followed in his footsteps as Britain's number one discus thrower.

Bill Tancred certainly took the discus event from comparative obscurity in Great Britain to true international class, and for more than a decade the Tancreds have been largely responsible for keeping us there. All three brothers are physical educationists and in this book Geoff couples his specialist skills and knowledge as a remedial gymnast to Bill's disciplined academic background as Director of Physical Education to Sheffield University.

The second good reason to support this work is my own constant feeling of responsibility to expand my own knowledge in a field of study in which I was intimately concerned more than fifteen years ago. In my own book on the subject I said then, and maintain still, that force or strength is as important to the explosive event athlete as breath is to the runner. What is more, whilst runners and coaches may argue over the relative merits of various running-based training programmes to improve performance, no one can seriously doubt the absolute specific need of weight training for the great majority of athletic events.

Therefore it behoves any of us who are in any way concerned with the improvement in performance in sport to heed the research, the added knowledge, the guidelines and conclusions reached in this book.

Ronald J Pickering, MEd, DPE

Acknowledgments

This book is largely the result of experience and knowledge gained as former international athletes and coaches of the British athletics team during the past twenty years.

We would like to express our sincere appreciation to a number of individuals who were of great assistance during the preparation and development of this manuscript:

to Adrian and Elsie Tancred, our parents, for their constant source of encouragement to take an active interest in all sports;

to Mrs Betty Bell and Mrs Val Tibenham who typed the whole of the manuscript we wish to record a special vote of thanks and appreciation for their excellent work;

to the Department of Physical Education and Sports Science, Loughborough University, for their co-operation in the use of the weight training room for the photographs;

to Sheffield University's Research Fund Grant;

to Adidas for their clothing worn for the photographs;

to Mr Ron Pickering, an eminent authority in sport, who has kindly written the foreword;

to our wives, Angela and Jane, for their understanding and patience whilst we pursued this manuscript;

to all sportsmen and sportswomen who kindly let us have their views on weight training for their respective sport;

finally, to Mr Eric Blackadder for the photographs illustrating the text and for the cover photograph.

Introduction

The last decade has seen a growing interest in physical fitness and its relationship to good health. Recent significant developments seem to indicate that a new era may be dawning for physical education as the public slowly becomes aware of the dangers of physical deterioration.

Most people can increase their strength, power, endurance, physical fitness and speed of movement by means of weight training, and there is no finer method of improving strength and power for all sports than by training with weights. However, irregular and haphazard training will not produce the desired results, and a training programme based on sound scientific principles is essential.

Speed of body movement is vital for success in any sport, and many people believe that there are various types of weight training exercises which can develop speed. Scientific research studies support this, and propose a programme of rapid lifting with light weights.

An obvious characteristic of the highly successful athlete is explosive power, resulting from a combination of the athlete's own strength and speed (or force and velocity). In scientific terms, power is the product of either speed or strength. For example, a small and relatively weak athlete can compensate for lack of strength with greater speed and so defeat much larger and stronger, but slower, competitors. Alternatively, a larger and slower athlete can compensate for lack of speed with greater strength, thereby defeating much speedier opponents. It must be emphasized that the most powerful athlete is the one who exhibits exceptional strength and speed. Such people normally have the ability to exert explosive bursts of muscular speed and are exceptionally strong.

A well-planned and scientifically-based weight training programme can develop strength and speed together, by overloading the muscle with sufficient weight to allow gains in strength, but not to such an extent that the muscle cannot be successfully contracted with an element of speed. This speed of movement can best be attained by fast exercising.

However, it must be pointed out that there are in various sports highly skilled men and women who are below the norm in strength and power. Such people seldom maintain their positions when faced with more powerful and equally skilled competitors. Naturally weight training needs to be adapted to particular sports, and of course the needs of all sports are different. For example, the squash player will try to gain muscular endurance, and the discus thrower will concentrate on strength development. It is therefore necessary that weight training schedules are adapted to meet individual requirements.

Today there is a real need for people involved in sport and physical fitness – teachers, coaches, students of sports science and participants – to have a better understanding of the true values of weight training. Many colleges, polytechnics and universities have included weight training courses in their sports studies and recreation curricula, and others will undoubtedly follow this trend. This book is designed to be especially useful to those following such courses, and to teachers, coaches, sports participants and keep fit fanatics in general.

Sheffield and Manchester, 1984

Bill Tancred and Geoff Tancred

1
The mechanics of muscles in action as applied to weight training

Hippocrates and Galen attempted to theorize the nature of muscular activity but it was not until the seventeenth century that any major progress was made when Antonj van Leeuwenhoek made the initial microscopic observation of muscle. His observations laid the foundations for today's understanding of the structure of muscles.

Muscles comprise approximately 45–50 per cent of the body's weight. On contraction, they effect movement of the body as a whole, including the circulatory vessels and respiratory, digestive and urinary tracts as well as the bones of the body for locomotion. The muscles' prime functions therefore are to contract and to create bodily movements.

Types of muscles

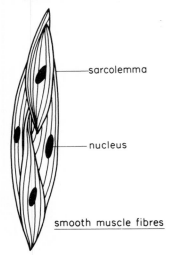

smooth muscle fibres

There are three types of muscle tissue, usually referred to as smooth, cardiac and striated. They are described below and illustrated in figure 1.

Smooth muscle is spindle-shaped and is under the control of the autonomic nervous system which cannot be influenced at will. It is found, for example, in the digestive tract and other hollow structures of the body.

Cardiac muscle is also involuntary but appears striated: the fibres intertwine to produce a continuous branching network, permitting the heart to contract rhythmically. The structure and function of cardiac muscle is peculiar to the heart. It responds to exercise and its condition and function can be improved with gradually progressive exercise of an endurance nature.

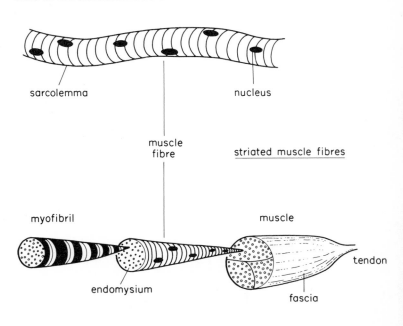

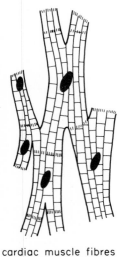

cardiac muscle fibres

Figure 1 Types of muscle tissue

Striated or *skeletal* muscles appear long and cylindrical with many crossbands or striations at regular intervals. These muscles are under voluntary control and are responsible for all bodily movements whether for sport, exercise or to conduct the general activities of daily living.

Since in order to participate in sport or exercises striated muscle is our main concern, it is perhaps wise to delve slightly deeper into its properties. A detailed description of striated muscle can be acquired from any major text on anatomy or physiology.

Motor unit

The basic unit of muscular contraction is the motor unit. This consists of a group of muscle fibres, each innervated by the terminal branches of a single motor axon (or motor nerve which directs impulses away from the brain). Motor units are subject to the *all-or-none* principle which means that the nerve fibres and associated muscle fibres respond entirely to a stimulus or do not respond at all. It is important to note that the individual motor unit does not determine the strength of contraction, but rather the number of motor units stimulated plus the rapidity of the stimulus govern the magnitude of contraction. Thus, the strength of muscle contraction is determined by the total number of motor units contracting and by the number of times per second each motor unit is stimulated.

Skeletal muscle tissue

Skeletal muscle tissue has three essential properties: *extensibility, elasticity* and *contractility*. Extensibility and elasticity may be compared to an elastic band; when a muscle is stretched it returns to its normal resting length once the stretching force has been discarded. Contractility is the peculiar property possessed by the whole tissue itself. Skeletal muscles are always maintained in a state of slight contraction, referred to as *muscle tone*, even if the muscles are not engaged in producing movement. This muscle tone is controlled by reflex actions due to the innervation of nerves and the presence of muscle spindles.

Origin and insertion

Muscles are penetrated by blood vessels and are supplied with nerves; they constitute the red meat of the body. All muscles are attached to bone either directly or by their connective tissue in the form of a *tendon* (a round cord or flat band) or an *aponeurosis* (fibrous sheet). Generally, muscle attachments are given the terms *origin* and *insertion*. The origin is that part of a muscle which remains relatively fixed during a movement under normal circumstances; in most cases it is the proximal attachment and is characterized by stability. Conversely, the insertion is that part of the muscle which moves a bone and is usually the distal attachment. Muscles do not, however, pull in one direction or the other. When a muscle contracts it exerts equal force on both its origin and insertion, attempting to pull its attachments towards each other. The nature of the exercise or movement will depend on which bone is to remain stationary and which one is to move.

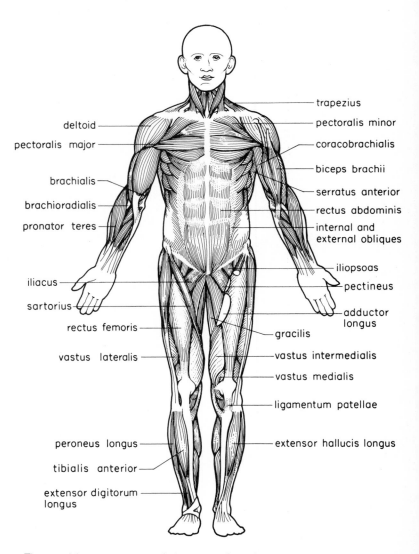

Figure 2 Major voluntary muscles (anterior view)

The quadriceps compose of the rectus femoris, vastus lateralis, vastus intermedialis and vastus medialis

Many bodily movements require the proximal bone (origin) to be stabilized or fixed while the distal bone (insertion) creates the desired movement. It is therefore apparent that another muscle or group of muscles must come into play to fix the bone of the origin attachment. This type of muscle action together with others will be described later under the heading 'Group action of muscles' (page 15). For co-ordinated movements, the mechanics of muscles in action involve an intricate and synchronised process, but to gain a clear understanding of muscle actions a concise knowledge of their attachments is necessary. Figures 2 and 3 illustrate the major skeletal muscles of the body.

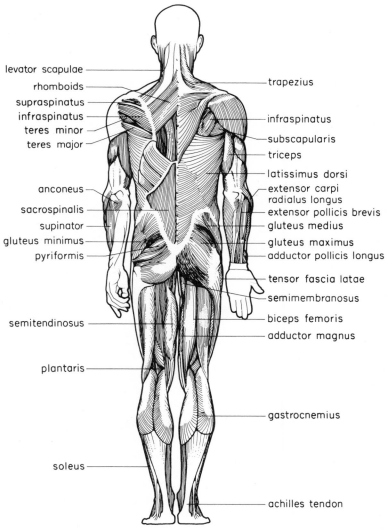

Figure 3 Major voluntary muscles (posterior view)

The erector spinae compose of the sacrospinalis and small muscles of the vertebral column

5

Types of muscle contraction

The term *contraction* refers to an increase in muscle tension. It does not, however, give an indication of any shortening taking place within a muscle. Muscular contractions are generally classified into different types based upon whether a muscle shortens, lengthens or remains relatively the same length when contracted. Muscles can engage in three types of contraction; these are *concentric* (shortening), *eccentric* (lengthening) and *static* (no change in muscle length).

Concentric contraction

This occurs when a muscle develops sufficient tension to overcome a resistance, thus causing a visible shortening, and movement of a body part. The muscle actively shortens and thickens with the insertion usually approaching the origin, since the latter is the more fixed or stabilized end. This is the type of muscle contraction usually seen in physical activities.

An example of concentric muscle work occurs when standing and bending the elbows to bring the hands to the chest (two arm bicep curl). In this case the resistance of the forearm and the effects of gravity have been overcome by the flexors of the elbow working concentrically; that is, shortening so that movement takes place.

Eccentric contraction

This type of contraction occurs when the origin and insertion of a muscle are drawn further apart under control, either by the effects of gravity or some other outside force. The muscle actually becomes longer and thinner, but still remains firm because it is working. A gradual releasing or 'letting-go' occurs either when gently lowering a weight under control or when the outside force is greater than the force of the contracting muscle. Although the term 'lengthening' is generally used to describe this type of muscle contraction, it means in fact that the muscle returns to its normal resting length from its shortened position. An example of eccentric muscle work occurs when standing and slowly lowering outstretched arms from the front to the side of the body.

Static contraction

This occurs when a muscle increases in tension but causes no appreciable joint movement. The length of the muscle remains the same, although either a maximal or sub-maximal contraction may be made. Static contractions can also occur when muscles antagonistic to each other contract with equal strength, balancing or counteracting each other.

An example of static muscle work would be to stand and hold the arms outstretched to the sides, horizontal to the ground. Static contractions can be made with gravity eliminated, for example, lying down tensing the quadriceps (the muscles on the front of the thighs) or against an outside force, for example, lying down and raising a single straight leg.

The term *isotonic* (equal tension) is often used to describe concentric contraction. The former occurs when a contraction is made whereby the tension remains the same as the muscle shortens. The latter term merely refers to a decrease in muscle length.

Isometric (equal length) contractions are often associated with static contractions. Isometric contractions are those which occur when a muscle is unable to shorten due to the magnitude of the resistance, as distinct from merely counterbalancing the effects of gravity. Only when static contractions involve maximal efforts are the two terms used synonymously.

Values of the type of muscle contraction for rehabilitation purposes

Concentric muscle work is widely used in rehabilitation schedules and fitness programmes to strengthen weak muscles. It is, however, the most difficult form of muscle work to produce since the muscles involved actively shorten and produce movement whilst overcoming a resistance or outside force.

Eccentric muscle work, from a rehabilitation point of view, is regarded as being easier than concentric work because it controls movements produced by some other force. This type of muscle work is extensively used in all phases of rehabilitation exercises. Muscles must be able to work eccentrically against a given force before they can work concentrically against the same force.

Static muscle work is considered to be the easiest form of muscle contraction and plays an important role in the early stages of remedial exercises. Static contractions are particularly important if one is encased in plaster. They enable muscle tone to be maintained during the period of fixation. Although it has been stated that static muscle work is the easiest to perform, it can also be the most tiring since fatigue products, such as lactic acid and carbon dioxide, collect and are less easily dissipated because the rate of circulation is not so rapid as in the other forms of muscle contraction.

Joint movement

When describing joint movement always consider the body in the 'anatomical position' which is standing with arms at the side of the trunk with the palms of the hands facing forward. Bodily movements can take place in different planes and axes.

Planes There are three different planes lying at right angles to each other, and they are illustrated in figure 4.

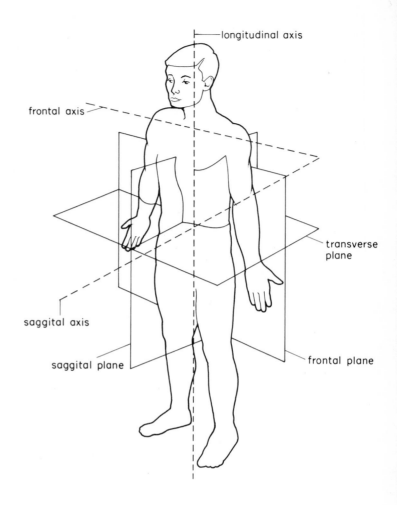

Figure 4 Anatomical position, planes and axes of the body

1 Sagittal plane
This is a vertical plane which passes through the body from front to rear as if bisecting it into two symmetrical halves. Forward and backward movements such as leaning forward, swinging arms backwards and bringing the knees to the chest are examples of movements in this plane.

2 Frontal plane
This is also a vertical plane but passes through the body from side to side (ear to ear), thus is at right angles to the sagittal plane. Examples of movements taking place in this plane are raising the arms sideways and side bending of the trunk.

3 Transverse plane
This is any horizontal plane which lies parallel to the diaphragm. Rotational movements take place in the transverse plane.

Axes   There are three types of axes used when describing bodily movements. An axis should be looked upon as a rod or pin passing through the body at right angles to a specific plane.

1 Frontal axis
This passes horizontally from side to side and is at right angles to the saggital plane. Therefore movements taking place in a sagittal plane move about a frontal axis.

2 Sagittal axis
This passes from front to rear lying at right angles to the frontal plane, so that movements taking place in a frontal plane move about a sagittal axis.

3 Longitudinal (or vertical) axis
This axis passes from the head to the feet, permitting rotational movements in a transverse plane.

Synovial joints and body movements

Synovial joints allow free movement, depending upon the structures forming and surrounding the joint. The fundamental movements of the body are varied and best described in relation to the planes, axes and anatomical position in which these movements occur. The various types of joint movement appear in figure 5.

Movements in the sagittal plane about a frontal axis

1 Flexion
The angle of a joint decreases (for example, bending the elbow).

2 Extension
The angle of a joint increases, and is thus the return movement from flexion (for example, straightening the knee).

Movements in the frontal plane about a sagittal axis

1 Abduction
Movement is away from the midline of the body (for example, raising the arms sideways).

2 Adduction
Movement is towards the midline of the body, and is thus the return from abduction.

3 Lateral flexion
This movement refers to side or lateral bending of the trunk and head.

4 Elevation
This movement refers to the raising of the shoulders

(shoulder shrugging) to develop the trapezius muscles. Such movements occur when cleaning a bar or during high pulls.

5 Depression
This is the opposite movement to elevation.

Movement in the transverse plane about a longitudinal axis

Rotation
This explains rotary movements of the trunk and head, and also includes inward and outward rotation of the shoulder joint.

The inward and outward rotation of the forearm are referred to as pronation and supination respectively.

Other important body movements

1 Circumduction
This refers to a combination of movements which occur in the sagittal and frontal planes involving flexion, abduction, extension and adduction. The movement which a body segment makes is described as a cone, with the apex at the joint and the base at the distal end of the moving part.

2 Supination
This is movement of the bones of the forearm permitting the palm to move forward or upwards so that the radius and ulna are parallel. This is usually done with the elbow fixed to eliminate any outward rotation of the shoulder joint.

3 Pronation
The opposite action to supination is pronation, thus the radius and ulna cross over each other.

4 Inversion
Movement permitting the sole of the foot to turn inwards.

5 Eversion
Movement permitting the sole of the foot to turn outwards.

6 Protraction
This allows a specific part of the body, such as the chin or shoulders, to move forward whilst other parts remain motionless.

7 Retraction
This allows for movement of a part of the body backwards, and is the opposite of protraction.

8 Dorsiflexion
Movement at the ankle permitting the toes to point towards the head or shin is known as dorsiflexion.

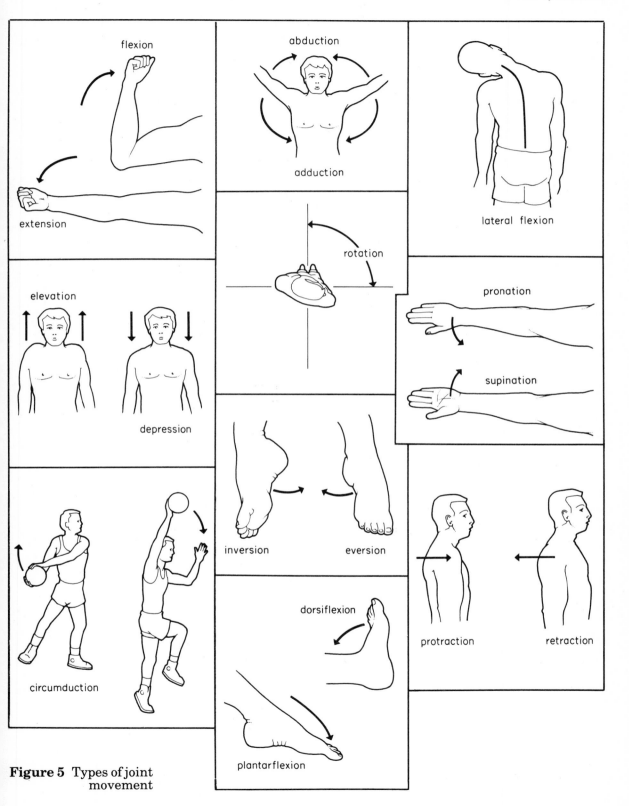

Figure 5 Types of joint movement

9 Plantarflexion
This is movement at the ankle permitting the toes to point away from the head.

Types of joints

People vary considerably in their range of motion or joint mobility and certain sports call for greater mobility than others. Various ways of measuring joint motion have been devised but the techniques lack uniformity. However, an individual's range of motion will depend on several factors including bone structure surrounding a joint, previous injury and previous training. The human body is composed of different types of joints; some are immovable (sutures in the skull); some are slightly movable (joints between the individual vertebrae); whilst others are more freely movable (synovial joints). It is this last type which is of interest to the weight trainer or sportsman or woman since these are the joints responsible for most forms of movement. Figure 6 illustrates the various types of joints in the human body.

Types of synovial joints

Synovial joints are divided into: plane, saddle, hinge, pivot, condyloid and ball and socket joints. Although all these joints are moved during most activities some are more active than others, depending on the nature of the task, exercise or sport.

Plane joints permit gliding movements such as those occurring in the small bones forming the wrist.

A *saddle* joint, of which there is only one true type in the body (carpometacarpal joint of the thumb) permits flexion, extension, abduction and adduction with a small degree of circumduction.

Hinge joints permit flexion and extension only, for example, the elbow joint.

Pivot joints permit rotary movements in a transverse plane about a longitudinal axis.

Condyloid joints allow small movements in flexion, extension, adduction, abduction and circumduction, and an example of this is the wrist joint. Condyloid joints are modified ball and socket joints.

Ball and socket joints allow a wide range of movements in flexion, extension, adduction and abduction, thus providing circumduction. The hip and shoulder joints are examples.

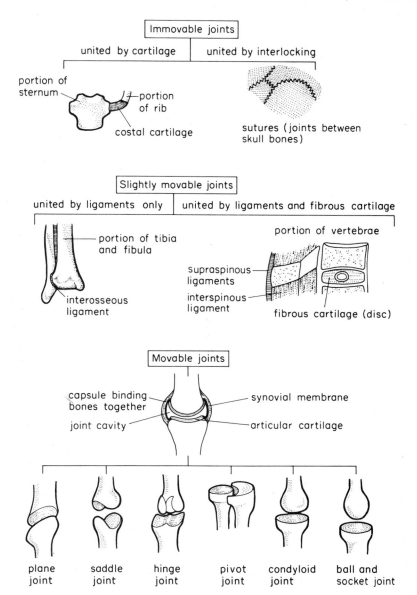

Figure 6 Types of joints in the human body

| plane joint | saddle joint | hinge joint | pivot joint | condyloid joint | ball and socket joint |

Ranges of motion

A great variety of exercises and degrees of movement can be performed due to the many joints in the body, but degree or range of motion will vary between individuals. These are described below and are illustrated in figure 7.

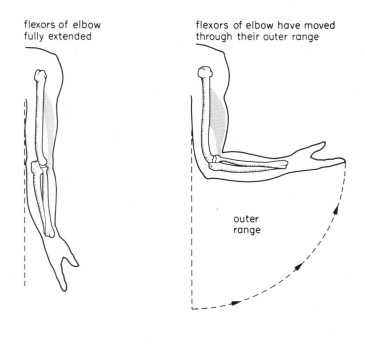

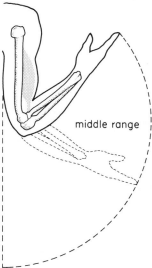

Figure 7 Ranges of muscle work

1 *Full range*
This occurs when a muscle contracts from its greatest possible lengthening to its greatest possible shortening.

2 *Outer range*
This is the distance a muscle works from a mid-point of the full range to its greatest possible lengthening.

3 Inner range

This occurs when muscle work is taking place from the mid-point of the full range to its greatest possible shortening.

4 Middle range

This is the middle third of the full range of movement.

A knowledge of the range of motion of certain joints can serve as an invaluable aid to training or even rehabilitation. Different sports call for certain muscles or joints to work in different ranges, and weight training exercises can be performed to concentrate either within a specified range of motion or in different ranges to maintain mobility, depending upon the requirements and nature of the exercise intended.

Exercises may be performed in a variety of ways by working on a combination of the ranges of motion. If a sportsperson requires muscular endurance for example, he or she may do six repetitions of an exercise in full range immediately followed by six repetitions in inner range and finally six repetitions in full range again. Any variation could be used with the different ranges of motion as well as the number of repetitions performed. Such a system of exercises is very demanding but good for the development of local muscular endurance.

Cases of stretched muscles, due to excessive twisting or stretching, can easily occur in sporting activities, and they can be shortened if worked concentrically and eccentrically in their inner range. Tight muscles, due to adaptive shortening or lack of regular activity, may be stretched to renew their habit length by working concentrically and eccentrically in their outer range. It is thus apparent that a knowledge and application of exercises in the different ranges of motion can have beneficial effects for everyone.

Group action of muscles

A muscle is capable of only two things: the development of tension within itself and relaxation; it very seldom acts alone. The term 'group action of muscles' indicates that any co-ordinated movement involves a synchronous act of several muscles working in a group or team. Any movement is caused by a muscle or group of muscles directly responsible for the movement itself; during that movement its opponents, or the muscles which produce the opposite effect, must relax sufficiently to allow the movement to occur. The muscles responsible for producing an effective movement must have a stable base and this is supplied by the bone not involved in the movement but which provides the attachment for one end of the muscle(s) directly responsible for the movement. This is explained more fully below under the heading 'Fixator'. Accordingly, some muscular activity is required to stabilize the bone serving as a stable base.

Many muscles act over more than one joint, and so many joints become movable during concentric or eccentric muscle work. However, in many cases only one joint may be required for a given exercise or movement, forcing another muscle group to work statically to prevent unnecessary joint action. Similarly, muscles acting over ball and socket joints may cause movements in more than one axis and yet movement in only one axis may be required for a specific action.

It should now be apparent that for well co-ordinated movements several muscles come into action, each playing various roles. Such actions are governed by the complex nature of the central nervous system and the cerebellum. Certain technical terms are used to describe various roles muscles may play. These are explained below, but first the terms 'origin' and 'insertion' should be revised (see page 3). The 'origin' is that part of the muscle attachment which remains relatively fixed during movement, whilst the 'insertion' is that part which moves.

1 Prime mover (or agonist)
This refers to muscles which are directly responsible for producing or controlling a specified joint action. An example of a prime mover in action is when the quadriceps contract against a resistance or outside force to straighten or extend the knee from a bent or flexed position.

2 Antagonist (or protagonist)
This is the name given to muscles which cause the opposite action from that of prime movers. In the above example of straightening the knee, the antagonists would be those muscles which cause the knee to bend, the hamstrings or knee flexors.

When the prime mover muscle contracts, its antagonists are reciprocally inhibited so that smooth, co-ordinated movements can take place. This is achieved by the muscles being reciprocally innervated so that when they contract their antagonists automatically relax. If this mechanism falters, especially during vigorous movements, strained or pulled muscles may occur.

3 Fixator (or stabilizer)
For effective and strong actions the prime mover must have a firm base upon which to pull. A muscle, when contracting, will tend to pull both of its end attachments towards its centre with equal force. But during most movements only one end of the muscle is required to move,

the insertion. Therefore, another muscle, or group of muscles, is required to work statically to stabilize, anchor, support or hold steady the bone to which the origin of the prime mover is attached. This is the function of the fixator.

Some, quite rare, actions involve muscles to work in reverse, which means the origin moving towards the insertion as in the case of chinning to the beam or heaving exercise, which is hanging freely at arm's length and pulling until the chin is in line or above the hands.

An example of a fixator action occurs when lying on the back with legs raised just clear of the floor and then gently lowered. The prime movers are the hip flexors, their origin primarily being on the pelvis and lumbar spine. The pelvis is, therefore, required to be fixed or stabilized so that effective performance of the hip flexors can take place. To do this the abdominal muscles work statically as fixators to steady the forward tilting of the pelvis.

4 Synergist (or neutraliser)

Many muscles act over two or more joints. In certain co-ordinated actions, not all the joints controlled by the prime mover may be required to move and a muscle or group of muscles is therefore required to prevent any undesired joint movement. For example, if a prime mover muscle flexes and rotates, but only rotation is required, an extensor muscle must work statically to counterbalance or neutralize the flexor action of the prime mover. The action of the extensor muscle is known as synergic muscle action and makes the prime mover more effective because the force of contraction is directed solely towards the desired action.

A prime example of synergic muscle action occurs when clenching the fist. The flexors of the fingers also flex the wrist joint. If all these joints were flexed a very feeble grip would ensue, for the tendons of the extensors are not long enough to permit full flexion of the fingers and wrist joint together. To produce a firm grip, therefore, the extensors of the wrist work statically as synergists to prevent any unwanted wrist flexion.

Regardless of the movement or exercise performed, it will be appreciated that a vast and complex network of muscular action takes place however simple the movement may appear. Often when people analyse a movement, or devise an exercise to develop a certain muscle group, only the prime movers are given consideration. Similarly, when attempting to define the action of a muscle, the many varied ways in which the muscle takes part is often overlooked. It must be remembered that all muscles come into action as part of a team of prime movers, antagonists, fixators and synergists.

Values of the group action of muscles

A knowledge of the group action of muscles will give a coach or sportsperson a better opportunity of selecting or devising an interesting and varied exercise programme. Too frequently boredom, staleness or lack of motivation exist in training schedules because of the narrow composition of exercises or activities performed. A wider variety may alleviate these problems and may result in a continued interest for training, possibly with further progress in strength, power and endurance.

Perhaps the greatest value served by a knowledge of the group action of muscles is recovery from injury. Sport injuries are becoming more frequent with the greater intensity and number of participants in sport today, and their very nature often poses difficulties in diagnosis and treatment due to their unique causes. An inherent trait among sportspeople is the desire not only to participate but also to compete, and injury prevents or limits this natural tendency. By competing or even only participating in a physical activity too soon after being injured, the injury may be aggravated and exacerbated, so delaying a complete return to sport.

An injury sustained is not an excuse for complete withdrawal from physical activity. Uninjured parts of the body can still be exercised, maintaining a degree of fitness and mobility. The injured area, however, requires more delicate and qualified treatment and the exercise therapy given will, of course, depend on the nature and severity of the injury as well as previous injury to the same area.

In the section describing the different types of muscle contraction (page 6) an explanation is given of their values for rehabilitation purposes, and it is perhaps advisable at this point to refer again to these notes.

If an injured muscle is too weak or painful to contract as a prime mover, it may be made to work statically as a fixator or synergist, even if the injured area has been immobilised by a plaster cast. A common injury among sportspeople, especially to footballers, is a torn cartilage. This injury prevents effective use of the quadricep muscles to extend the knee joint. To restore or maintain muscle tone and strength, however, the quadriceps can be made to work statically either as fixators or synergists. The quadriceps will work statically as fixators to steady the pelvis in the following exercise: lie on the floor with the feet held under the wall bars or by a partner and, with the arms behind the head, sit up.

In the following exercise the quadriceps work as synergists: lie face downwards (prone) and raise a single leg upwards, keeping it straight throughout the movement. The prime movers here are the hamstrings, but these form a muscle group which acts over two joints. Firstly, they extend the hip, as is required in the exercise described, and secondly they flex or bend the knee, a movement not required for this specific exercise. Therefore, to prevent unnecessary joint movement, in this case flexion of the knee, the quadriceps work synergically to keep the knee straight.

Levers

All body movements occur by means of a system of levers. An understanding of the principle of leverage and the various kinds of levers is essential for comprehending the movements of the body. A lever may be defined as a rigid bar capable of turning about a fixed point (called a fulcrum or axis). In the human body, the bones represent the bars or levers, and the joints the fulcrums or axes. The weight is the resistance to be moved, whether it be a limb or additional weight. (The effects of gravity should also be taken into account.) The contraction of muscles provides the force or power to move the lever.

There are three main types of lever, named according to the arrangement of the *fulcrum* (F), *power* (P) and *weight* (W). The term power is sometimes substituted for the words force or effort, and weight for resistance. The former terms with their abbreviations will be used here (see figure 8).

There are three possible arrangements of the three elements of a lever. Any one of these three elements may be situated between the other two. The arrangement or relative position of the elements provides the basis for the classification of levers, referred to as the first, second and third class or order of levers. These are shown diagramatically in figure 8.

Two important terms need clarifying. The *weight arm* (WA) is the part of the lever between the F and W, and the *power arm* (PA) is the part of the lever between the F and P. The longer the PA, the easier the movement and, therefore, the smaller the amount of effort required. The longer the WA, the more difficult it will be to make the movement and, therefore, the greater the effort which is required.

In the *first order* of levers the F is between the P and W, situated centrally or towards either the P or W; and either the PA or WA may be longer than the other depending upon the location of the F along the lever. As a consequence, the two arms of the lever move in opposite directions. Such a lever often sacrifices force to gain speed. An example of this type of lever is that of a seesaw.

The *second order* of levers has the W between the F and P. The PA will always be longer than the WA. Here speed

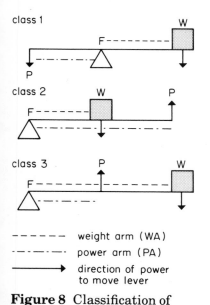

class 1

class 2

class 3

— — — — — weight arm (WA)
— · — · — power arm (PA)
———▶ direction of power
to move lever

Figure 8 Classification of levers

is sacrificed to gain power. An example of this type of lever is lifting a wheelbarrow.

In the *third order* of levers the P lies between the F and W. The WA will always exceed the PA. An example of this type of lever is a spring used for closing a fire door.

Mechanical advantage (MA)

The MA of any lever (or machine) is the relationship between the PA and WA. The greater the length of the PA relative to the WA, the greater the MA; that is, less effort will be required to perform the task. A MA is obtained in the first order of levers when the F is nearer to the W than to the P, and in all second order of levers. It is never obtained in levers of the third order since these work at a mechanical disadvantage.

Levers in the human body

Several examples are generally cited as resembling the different types of levers in the human body. Some of these are only listed below, for detailed explanations can be obtained from many major texts on anatomy and physiology.

First order

1. Nodding of the head.
2. Elbow extension as in the case of the bent arm pullover exercise, described on page 75.
3. Plantarflexing the ankle with the foot off the ground.

Second order

Many authorities believe that there are no true second order levers within the human body. However, the following have been described to indicate this type of lever:
1. Heel raising.
2. Flexion of the elbow due to the brachioradialis muscle.

Third order

This is the most common class of lever in the human body; examples are:
1. Flexion of the elbow due to the action of the biceps and brachialis.
2. Knee extension by the quadriceps.
3. Knee flexion by the hamstrings.

Practical application of levers

Much can be done to change the length of the WAs in the human body but nothing can be done to change the length of PAs. As levers are lengthened by extending at certain joints, greater potential for speed and range of movement occurs at the end of the lever, or at any point along it. When the lever is shortened by flexing at certain joints, greater potential to exert force occurs.

Many sports use implements to gain an advantage of speed at the expense of power. These would include tennis rackets, hockey sticks, baseball bats, golf clubs, fencing foils, squash and badminton rackets. The length of the implements enables their ends to travel through a large arc of motion and at speed.

Certain exercises can be made more difficult by lengthening the lever. The following are some general examples:

1 Abducting the shoulders with the elbows flexed, and gradually progressing until the movement can be performed with the arms straight.

2 Lying, raising the knee to the chest allowing the knee to bend, then keeping the leg straight and flexing the hip as far as possible.

3 Holding a weight near to the chest, then gradually straightening the arms until the same weight can be held with the arms outstretched.

2
Safety factors in weight training

Weight training is only hazardous when carelessness and ignorance replace good judgement and common sense. If monitored properly and with the correct application of training principles weight training can be one of the safest physical activities.

This chapter concentrates on the safety aspect of the sport and discusses the role of the teacher or coach in maintaining appropriate standards for a weight training programme.

Progress in the scientific development of muscle size and strength, through the use of progressive resistance, has at times been retarded by claims of the dangers inherent in exercise of this nature. It has been said that the likelihood of becoming 'muscle bound' and the probability of incurring a hernia are increased. However, recently the results of carefully controlled investigations have helped immensely to convince the sceptics that this is not the case. Virtually everyone can benefit enormously from weight training.

It may be that there are certain dangers in resistance exercises but these seem less likely to lie with the exercise *per se*, as with unsafe situations arising out of poorly organised and poorly administered programmes of weight training.

Performing area   The performing area in which the lifting takes place is extremely important for the safe conduct of any weight training programme and should this space be too small, there may be a high risk of accidents happening. Top weight trainers advocate that the minimum area allowable for each person to perform an exercise with a barbell in safety should be no less than 2 metres square. This is especially important for the safe performance of supine exercises, and the squat. In a crowded environment there is a real danger of a person being jostled or pushed whilst in the supine position holding a heavy bar directly over the head, or dropping or falling with a loaded bar whilst performing the squat may result in permanent injury to the back or knees.

It is evident that it is much safer to perform an exercise in an adequate area, particularly when balance is of prime importance in the execution of the lift.

Lighting   Although from a strict safety viewpoint the provision of sufficient lighting (natural or artificial) need not be given the same consideration as a sufficiently large area, it will contribute enormously to the success of the weight training programme.

It is often the case that weight training and weight lifting activities are assigned to the smallest, darkest and dingiest of places. This has understandably done very little to help the status of these sports in the public eye. Today, however, this state of affairs is improving and, in many places, better facilities are being provided so that people can train and exercise in a conducive sporting environment.

Ventilation The wisdom of a well-ventilated room or area for weight training is self-evident although this is not in itself a safety practice. The atmosphere can become most unpleasant if weight training is performed in a poorly ventilated area, particularly when some of the heavy exercises require deep or forced inhalation.

Floor surface The polished gymnasium floor, with a slick and hard surface, would probably not be considered dangerous for the majority of exercises commonly practised in weight training programmes. Exceptions, possibly, might be squats and certain so-called dynamic lifts, for example the snatch, when heavy weights are used. However, since weight training and weight lifting are often practised together, the surface of the training area should be looked at carefully.

Ideally, the floor surface for weight training, from a safety and maintenance viewpoint, should be concrete covered by rubber matting and for Olympic lifting a wooden platform should be placed on top of the matting. This would be safer and more economical in the long term in that the floor and rubber matting are protected by the platform.

Equipment considerations

Over the past decade the equipment used in weight training has been standardized by governing bodies throughout the world. This applies to the bar lengths both for barbells and dumb-bells; diameters, weight of bars and material utilized; plate sizes and construction; and types of inside and outside collars and their construction. A certain uniformity extends into the construction of other pieces of apparatus, for example, racks for storing barbells, dumb-bells and additional plates; abdominal and inclined boards; various pulley devices and racks or supports for exercises like the squats.

Quality From a safety viewpoint it is important to remember that the quality most essential to any of the paraphernalia of weight training programmes is strength. A considerable contribution to the overall safety standards of weight training apparatus has been made with the use of solid steel stock, instead of iron pipe in the construction of barbell and dumb-bell bars, and the use of steel shafting or heavy gauge pipe in place of wood for bench legs and supports, squat stands and pulley device supports.

Naturally, the equipment employed in any weight training programme must be constructed in such a way that it is safe for all users. It is essential, to avoid as many accidents during the training programme as possible, that regular and careful inspections are made of all the equipment used, and that any repair work necessary is carried out immediately. Equipment left in a poor condition can be dangerous and can cause permanent injury.

Administrative considerations

Weight training programmes should be very carefully thought out in order to avoid accidents. Poor and unprofessional methods of organizing groups, with little or no attention to the details of class size, available area or necessary equipment will result in a potentially dangerous situation. Probably few, if any, of the desired objectives will be achieved.

From an organizational viewpoint, and with the safety element in mind, it is wise to divide groups or classes into units of two, three or four individuals. As far as possible each participant should be of about the same height and weight. Of course the size or number in each unit will depend on the availability of space and equipment. Weight training partners assume almost the same importance as the 'spotters' in gymnastics, in that they provide assistance when needed. Occasionally situations arise in the course of performing an exercise with weights in which immediate assistance is necessary for the prevention of injury. This is particularly true of two popular exercises, the bench press and the squat. The use of relatively heavy weights in these lifts and the balance factor involved make spotters particularly important and essential.

Instruction and supervision considerations

Weight training injuries and accidents can be minimized among individuals and groups who have had meticulous and sound instruction in every phase of each exercise and in the correct procedure to adopt when using different items of apparatus and equipment. The extreme necessity of attention to detail in the correct execution of each exercise, and the definitely secondary importance of the amount of weight used, must be stressed to the lifter during the beginning instructional part of any weight training programme.

However, detailed instruction without sufficient follow-up supervision is valueless. Although the lifter may be supplied with first-class initial instruction in a programme designed to accomplish certain objectives, the quality of the subsequent guidance given by the coach or teacher will determine their ultimate success.

It appears that preventable accidents often occur in (even temporarily) unsupervised classes. Weight training requires an unusually high degree of supervision as compared with many other sports and physical activities which may be partially or completely self-maintained. The following points illustrate the importance of the attendance of the coach or teacher during the weight training class.

1 Correct technique and good body position should be stressed at all times.

2 All weights lifted from the floor should be lifted using the legs as the primary force, while keeping the back flat.

3 It is just as easy to hurt oneself by putting down a weight wrongly as it is to lift incorrectly in the first instance.

4 Increase in kilogrammes should be gradual.

5 Fooling around the performing area should be stopped immediately.

6 Correct breathing on all lifts must be taught and supervised, especially in the initial stages of learning to train with weights.

Some physiological dangers

1 The importance of the warm-up

Most coaches, sportsmen and sportswomen believe that a warm-up session is valuable and essential, but some physiologists claim otherwise. However, until all physiologists agree, we strongly advocate that a thorough warm-up is carried out prior to any physical activity. Many experts claim, and we agree with them, that failure to warm up may lead to the tearing of muscle fibres.

The warm-up should be specific to the activity to be performed and should be increased in intensity as the performer becomes better conditioned. The timing of the warm-up in relation to the performance must be correct otherwise the beneficial effects may be reduced or eliminated. It is important that the warm-up should include some stretching and loosening exercises along with some heavy work; this will help to minimize injuries, enabling sportsmen and women to train harder and longer without interruptions in their training schedules. (See table 1, page 34.)

2 Muscle-boundness

Among the numerous criticisms with which weight training has been charged, is that it slows down sportsmen and women, making them muscle-bound. Muscle-boundness is when the full range of movement is shortened and, therefore, sports performance deteriorates.

However, informed articles and periodicals have proved the reverse; weight training does not produce muscle-boundness but helps to improve physical performance. Additionally, many people who have practised the sport of weight training for many years feel that it has enhanced their range of speed and movement.

Quite clearly, the traditional misconceptions relating to muscle-boundness have been neutralized by the enormous amount of scientific evidence of recent years.

3 Hernia

One of the primary objections to weight training, from a safety viewpoint, has always been the fear of incurring a hernia or aggravating an existing one. It must be pointed out that there are no indications of a higher incidence of herniation or rupture among those participating with weights than among those taking part in any other form of strenuous physical activity.

Anyone with a predisposition to this condition, that is, a repaired hernia, diagnosed unrepaired hernia, or a known or suspected weakness of the abdominal musculature, should not participate with weights unless given approval by someone in the medical profession, and should then proceed only cautiously. The tension developed when exerting maximum effort for optimum results in weight training effects an increase in intra-abdominal pressure that may contra-indicate this type of exercise for those in the above category. An examination by a medical doctor prior to any weight training activities should reveal any such weakness.

Additionally, the basic principles that govern safe lifting of any heavy object should be given the strictest attention in order to reduce the possibility of injury.

4 The valsalva phenomenon

The *valsalva phenomenon*, named after an Italian anatomist, Antonio Valsalva (1666–1723), is characterized by a voluntary attempt to exhale forcibly against a closed glottis (opening of the upper part of the windpipe). This effort involves a shortening contraction of the diaphragm muscle, the abdominal muscle group and the muscles which lower the rib cage. Any exercise involving the big muscle groups (for example, the legs) and requiring maximum effort will undoubtedly result in high degrees of tension. The weight training participant often holds his or her breath during such exercises, causing pressure within the chest cavity to rise markedly. Heart output and arterial pressure increase significantly and the inhibited venous return causes a drop in blood pressure. When the exercise is completed blood pressure may rise considerably above normal as the heart is again surcharged with blood.

As a result, maximum exertion during exercises for development of the big muscle groups would be unsafe, or at least require extreme caution in administration, for those having circulorespiratory weaknesses or for the aged. However, the average weight trainer rarely reaches the limits of exertion and so the effects of the valsalva phenomenon would be only a secondary safety consideration.

Summary

Scientific research into and experience of the various aspects of progressive resistance exercise, particularly during the last decade, seem to highlight the advantages of exercise of this type which far outweigh the disadvantages. Traditionally, objections to weight training have centred around the inadvisability of the practice from a physical safety viewpoint. An assortment of injuries, temporary and permanent, have been forecast for those choosing to participate in both weight training and weight lifting activities but recent investigations have shown ways by which likely dangers inherent in the sport may largely be curtailed.
Some of the safety codes of practice are set out below:

a The weight training room must be large enough for the participants to perform comfortably and should be well lighted and well ventilated, with a floor surface rough enough to reduce the possibility of slipping and falling.

b The equipment should be well constructed and well maintained, with regular and thorough inspections for unsafe features.

c The strictest attention should be given to detail during the instructional and supervisory phases of the weight training programme.

d There should be sufficient time for a thorough warm-up prior to the lifting of weights, so as to prevent trauma to the body structures involved.

e Exercise movements should be performed through the full range of movement to effect the most complete stretching of the muscles and their tendons.

f Weight trainers should undergo a thorough physical examination in order to determine cardiac, abdominal or other weaknesses which would be aggravated by exercising with weights, particularly after injury or at the beginning of a new season.

Limited space precludes us from going into more detail of how to administer a safe and successful weight training programme. Even so, if people interested in weight training, whether coach or performer, follow the guidelines on safety precautions discussed in this chapter, the accident and injury rate for weight training will be no more, and probably lower, than that for any other physical activity or sport.

3
The development of the
weight training programme

We should like to begin by stressing that anyone interested in developing a weight training programme should seek the help and guidance of a qualified teacher or instructor of weight training approved by the British Amateur Weight Lifting Association (BAWLA).*

1 Equipment

The first step when planning a weight training programme is to check the amount of equipment available and work out the needs of the participants. Then, make sure that all the equipment is up to standard, and if more is needed, buy apparatus that will stand the rigours of heavy usage.

The basic equipment depends entirely on the type of programme planned. There should generally be sufficient equipment in the gymnasium for every individual in training to work to his or her maximum. It is most frustrating for a participant to have to wait several minutes doing absolutely nothing before the next set of exercises. Long periods of inactivity help no one.

For a group of thirty participants we suggest that ten bars with collars would be needed, plus twenty 2½ kilogramme discs, twenty 5 kilogramme discs, forty 7½ kilogramme discs, as well as a few heavier discs, squat stands, racks and benches.

2 Performing area

As was said earlier (page 24), participants should be able to perform in an environment in which they feel that they want to train hard. The performing area is of paramount importance if individuals are to progress and attend the training sessions regularly.

Sometimes the performing area is the corner of a sports hall or an unused building like a garage, but ideally it should be separate from the sports hall or gymnasium, and located in a room of its own. Weight training can then be performed comfortably without distractions from outsiders.

There are several ways to organize the weight training room. An arrangement used by Sheffield University for both weight training and weight lifting is shown in figure 9.

* BAWLA General Secretary, 3 Iffley Turn, Oxford.

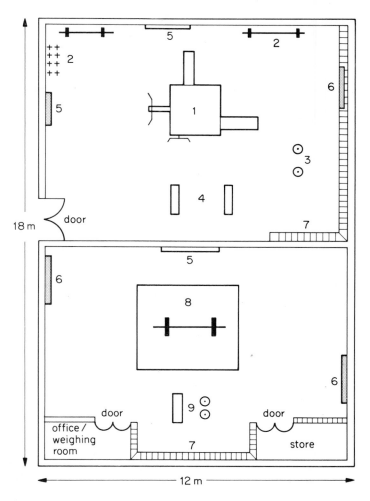

Figure 9 Plan of the weight training and lifting room

1 multigym
2 storage racks for individual weights
3 free standing squat stands
4 free standing adjustable benches
5 full length mirrors
6 noticeboards
7 fixed bench seating
8 4m x 4m sectional timber platforms and Olympic bar with weights
9 free standing heavy duty adjustable bench and squat stands

3 Warm-up prior to lifting

The question of the warm-up must be considered in the development of the weight training programme. As was noted on page 27 it is important that, before any weights are lifted, a thorough warm-up session is carried out. This may be in the form of general stretching exercises and running. The warm-up should increase blood circulation and will prepare the sportsperson for the weight training task ahead.

A simple but effective warm-up session of stretching and running is outlined in table 1.

Table 1

Order of exercise	Type of exercise	Sets	Repetitions
1	Quarter mile run (slow)	1	1
2	Side bends	2	10 (each side)
3	Bending forwards to touch the floor (with legs straight)	2	10
4	Jump squats	2	10
5	Pressing arms and shoulders backwards (arms straight)	2	10
6	Press-ups (chest to the floor)	2	8–12

Note

The terms used in the tables in this book might not be immediately understood by the reader, and are explained below.

Repetitions (Reps) – the number of times an exercise or lift is performed without stopping.

Sets – a specified number of repetitions constitutes one set. Two sets of five repetitions is written as 2×5.

Kilogrammes – all weights used in this book are in kilogrammes. One kilogramme is equal to 2.2046 pounds and a conversion table can be found in the Appendix on page 132.

Figure – represents the number of the exercise displayed in chapter 4.

The weights suggested in this book are meant only as a guide and adjustments up or down may be necessary. No distinction is made between youths and adults, both being treated in the beginner category. However, where adults are obviously stronger than youths, additional weight can be used, but it is important that this is left to the discretion of the coach or teacher.

If light weight training is used following a session of stretching and running, exercises involving full body movement with speed and power are strongly recommended, and table 2 suggests a suitable programme. The exercises are described in full in chapter 4 (pages 53–84). It is often worth while for a teacher or coach to spend the first two or three periods with a beginners' class leading the warm-up procedure. Once this procedure has been mastered, the class can then move on to the actual lifting of weights.

Table 2

Order of exercise	Type of exercise (power lifts)	Sets	Reps	Kilogrammes		Figure
				Men	Women	
1	High pulls	2	5	15	7½	22
2	Cleans	2	5	20	10	17
3	Military press	2	5	15	7½	25
4	Snatch	2	5	20	10	18

4 Starting weight

It is sometimes felt that the weight used at the beginning of the weight training programme should be dependent upon the type of benefit required (for example, muscular strength or muscular endurance), but we believe otherwise. We feel that the starting weight should be very low as it is important in the initial stages of weight training to learn the correct technique of lifting. Only when this technical aspect has been mastered can individual specialization take place.

The starting weight does depend, however, entirely on the individual but very often the optimum weight is found only on a trial and error basis. At present there is no sound scientific method to determine the starting weight for any weight training exercise. The simplest way, although not perfect by any means, is based on an analysis of body weight and physique. These two factors can serve as an estimate of strength and can help in getting the participants started. This method is illustrated in table 3, and assumes that the participant is a complete novice but healthy and relatively fit.

Table 3

Order of exercise	Type of exercise	Proposed starting weight	Figure
1	Military press	⅓ body-weight	25
2	Sit-ups	—	—
3	Bench press	½ body-weight	31
4	Back squat	½ body-weight	38
5	Curls	⅓ body-weight	28

As a point of interest, if body-weight is used to establish the starting weight for the programme, the overweight participant will often find that the load is too heavy. Some sympathy should be given to the lifter and the weight reduced. However, the following method is probably the best one for ascertaining the optimum starting weight for each individual. The class is divided into groups of four and each group is allotted a position at one of the various exercises that are to be attempted. The class should then be given a clear demonstration of how to count and change the weights on a weight training bar correctly. Each group should take all the weight off the bar at their particular exercise station.

Next the class should be given a demonstration of an exercise: for example, the military press (page 63, figure 25). Each participant can then practise the exercise with no weight at all on the bar so as to perfect the technique. Two members of the group should hand the bar to a third at chest level (chest rest position, page 52) while the fourth member rests. In this way each member of the group has a short rest whilst waiting for his or her next turn.

Once the groups have mastered the technique of the exercise, weights can be added to the bar in 5 kilogramme stages, and the participants can begin to train with weights. When they have lifted as much as they can, they must remember the weight lifted but continue to help with the bar until all the members of the group have reached their maximum lift. At this point the coach or teacher records the successful maximum lift of each individual.

An alternative method of discovering each person's maximum lift is to load the weight training bars in 5 kilogramme intervals at different exercise positions around the performing area. After a thorough warm-up, with a demonstration and explanation of the exercise, the participants, starting at the lightest weight, move around the exercise stations, performing the required lift. Eventually, as participants proceed up the weight scale, they will no longer manage a proper lift, and so the maximum weight lifted can be recorded by the teacher or coach at the last bar lifted correctly. We strongly recommend that no individual should attempt any lift during the testing procedure alone. Beginners, and even experts, can find themselves stuck with a heavy bar causing discomfort, which may result in permanent injury.

The weight training programme of each individual must be planned carefully on the results of his/her own maximum lift. It is recommended that a high repetition programme of light weights is planned for the first few training sessions. An extremely popular method amongst beginners for starting at a comfortable weight is to take half of the participant's maximum lift weight and perform one set of ten repetitions at this weight, before adding 5 kilogrammes and performing a set of eight repetitions. Finally, add another 5 kilogrammes and perform a final set of six repetitions. For example, if a participant's maximum first military press is 50 kilogrammes, the first set of ten repetitions would be at 25 kilogrammes, followed by a set of eight repetitions at 30 kilogrammes, and a third set of six repetitions with 35 kilogrammes. As the amount of weight increases, the number of repetitions decreases. (Each exercise should involve three sets of ten, eight and six repetitions respectively.). Calculations for each participant on the basis of the four basic lifts mentioned in table 3 can be made for the whole weight training programme.

Illustrated in tables 4 and 5 are two examples of a beginner's programme.

Table 4 – Men

| Order of exercise | Type of exercise | Maximum lift | Half of maximum lift | Starting weight | | | Figure |
				Reps 10	Reps 8	Reps 6	
1	Military press	50	25	25	30	35	25
2	Back squat	60	30	30	35	40	38
3	Curls	30	15	15	20	25	28
4	Bench press	60	30	30	35	40	31

Table 5 – Women

Order of exercise	Type of exercise	Maximum lift	Half of maximum lift	Reps 10	Reps 8	Reps 6	Figure
1	Military press	25	12½	12½	15	17½	25
2	Back squat	30	15	15	20	25	38
3	Curls	15	7½	7½	10	12½	28
4	Bench press	30	15	15	20	25	31

It is very likely that some individuals will make faster progress than others in terms of speed and strength in lifting. If this is the case it is better to concentrate on the technique of lifting and not rush into heavy lifting. A beginner's programme set at a lower weight rather than one set too high will pay off in the long run.

Other starting methods might be implemented to suit individual needs. For example, participants may be divided into groups as suggested previously and asked to perform a lift ten times instead of once. When the lift has been performed correctly by each participant, weight is added to the bar and the lift is performed eight more times. The participants continue adding further weights and decreasing the repetitions until they can no longer improve. Naturally, the other exercises are performed in similar fashion. (Note that the suggested starting weight for a particular exercise is when the participant can perform 10 repetitions correctly.) Although this method takes more time than the others already discussed, it is on the whole much safer and more reliable because progress can be monitored more easily.

Once the starting weight has been calculated for each participant, it should be recorded and kept in a place for all to see. The record sheet should look like that illustrated in table 6. A clear advantage of a weight training programme is that progress can be achieved with relative ease. If the record sheets are kept up to date, any progress made can easily be seen and as a result interest and enthusiasm will be maintained.

Table 6 Weight training record sheet

Weight training for sport record sheet

Name... Sport...

Type of exercise	Date			Date			Date			Date...... Best ever lift
	Sets	Reps	Kg	Sets	Reps	Kg	Sets	Reps	Kg	

Key Sets – number of sets
Reps – number of repetitions
Kg – amount of weight lifted in
      kilogrammes

Signature...
coach/teacher

5 Exercise arrangement and selection procedure

The exercises in a weight training programme should be chosen to suit the needs of the individual. For example, a shot putter will need to exercise those muscles that propel the shot a long way, whereas a basketball player will need to develop those muscles that will give the ability to jump higher than the opponents.

However, it should be said that the development of the general musculature should be pursued first before concentrating on specific muscle groups relating to an individual's particular sport.

Many weight training exercises will develop and strengthen the human body but naturally there is only time and energy to perform a very small number of these. As a result, this small number must be selected very carefully. The five weight training exercises and the sit-ups in table 7 are generally considered to be quite basic and will help most beginners to develop strength.

Table 7 A programme for beginners

Order of exercise	Type of exercise	Sets	Reps	Kilogrammes		Development area of body	Figure
				Men	Women		
1	Warm-up	(schedule as described earlier)					—
2	Military press	2	10	20	10	Shoulders	25
3	Curls	2	10	12½	7½	Upper arms	28
4	Back squat	2	10	25	12½	Legs	38
5	Bench press	2	10	25	12½	Upper chest/arms	31
6	Dead lift	2	6	45	22½	Legs/back	37
7	Sit-ups	3	15	No weight		Abdominals	—

This programme for beginners will develop the major muscle groups of the body and the exercises are tabulated so that no two exercises working the same muscle groups follow in succession. This arrangement ensures sufficient recovery time for the participant who will otherwise become fatigued quite quickly.

We must stress that this programme is meant only as a guide and other exercises can be substituted to suit individual needs and requirements.

6 Selection procedure for the training groups

It is probably wise to divide participants, as far as possible, into homogeneous groups. For example, if strength is the criterion used, then the strongest participants will be in one group, the next strongest in another group and so on. The coach or teacher should explain the method used and this will then serve as a motivating force for the class to progress rapidly, in order to move into a stronger group. However, it is important to remember that these are ability groups and ability should change. If efficient organization is to be maintained the groups should only be altered either at the beginning or at the end of a training session by the coach or teacher.

Once the participants have been grouped according to strength, weight training record sheets should be given to the leader of each group, who will then be responsible for them. Any changes made to the record sheets should be sanctioned by the coach or teacher first. Efficient class organization should enable the coach or teacher to spend most of his or her time giving guidance and encouragement.

Finally, it is important that (after a thorough warm-up) the participant using the least amount of weight for each exercise begins the programme. This will ensure smooth progress within each group and safeguard the precious time that is allocated to weight training.

7 Duration of training time to obtain satisfactory results

Most people can attain maximum strength and power if they train conscientiously with weights for a relatively short period, and all programmes should be planned with this in mind. In most instances, particularly at school level, the time given to weight training is relatively short, so it is imperative that participants perform in a sensible manner. The shorter the exercise period, the more crucial it becomes that it is properly organized to ensure that the lifting time is used to its full advantage. An adequate training session can be conducted in approximately thirty to forty minutes but, ideally, for a person to take maximum advantage the training session should be about sixty minutes.

The coach or teacher organizing the programme must decide on the percentage of the maximum load to be attempted, the number of repetitions and sets, and the amount of time that is required between sets to recover sufficiently.

There are two schools of thought today regarding the scope of the beginner's exercise programme. One recommends that a wide variety of exercises should be included and that only one set of each be performed during each training session. This type of programme has a great advantage if time is not important. The other school of thought recommends that only a few basic exercises should be performed in the training session, using three sets for each exercise. Incorporating basic exercises into such a programme enables the participant to concentrate on the lifts which exercise the major muscle groups and requires less time in changing weights on the bar. How-ever, a combination of the two training programmes would be the best plan.

The following routine should serve as an example. On Monday, perform three sets of ten, eight and six repetitions of only a few basic exercises. The Wednesday programme should involve a variety of exercises but only one set of each performed. Then on Friday, perform Monday's schedule again but this time with slightly heavier weights.

Any muscle group that is worked extremely hard for a short duration of time requires a period of rest before it is asked to work hard again. A rest of two to three minutes will normally suffice but this does depend on the individual's physical fitness and the load being attempted. We recommend that weight training for beginners should take place on alternate days so that there is a sufficient recovery period between lifting sessions. Another reason for this is that on 'rest' days agility and specific skill development can be attempted. This is particularly relevant for sportsmen and sportswomen who use weight training only as an aid to the development of their own sport.

8 Progress

It is helpful to beginners if they practise their starting programme of three sets of ten, eight and six repetitions of each exercise for about two weeks. This allows them to become accustomed to the correct application of the exercise and the general overall feel of lifting light weights.

Only when participants can perform the repetitions and sets comfortably and technically well, should they proceed to a higher weight. For example, imagine that the participant is on a ten, eight, six repetition schedule of 35, 40 and 45 kilogrammes respectively. When a weight trainer is proficient at lifting 45 kilogrammes ten times, he then is allowed to change the weights to 40, 45 and 50 kilogrammes. When the 50 kilogrammes can be lifted successfully ten times on the third set, the weights may be changed to 45, 50 and 55 kilogrammes.

Once the participant has been lifting for about a month, it is worth while occasionally lowering the number of repetitions in each set so that heavier loads can be attempted. A schedule of this nature is a good way to break the same routine and provides the occasional maximum overload which muscles need for maximum strength gains. This is called the pyramid method of training. In practice what happens is that the repetitions are decreased but the weight increased until the lifter can no longer perform that lift properly.

As always rapid progress can be expected in the initial stages of training. One of the reasons for this is that the participants are frequently started on a weight training programme using only token weights and so they will be keen to reach the weight lifting levels which they consider they should achieve. Other reasons for rapid progress include the mastering of the technical aspects of lifting and, naturally, an increase in strength.

Sooner or later, the participant will reach a 'sticking point', or what is termed a *plateau*, beyond which it seems impossible to progress. When this happens the training routine should be altered and, occasionally, it helps to cease weight training altogether for a period of three days or so. Other methods of overcoming this 'menace' have been tried by coaches and trainers, and one successful way we use is to select a weight below that at which the participant is experiencing difficulties, and perform the same repetitions and sets. After about two weeks of practising the same routine, participants are generally able to progress beyond their previous barrier. However, it must be stressed that the better lifter you are, the harder it is to beat this plateau level.

9 Weight training rest days

Many top class sports competitors, particularly during the competitive season, have at least one day off during the week in which they perform no physical activity at all. They need this rest day to recover and remain sharp for the competition that lies ahead.

Beginners of weight training also need some rest days but it is difficult to state how many because of individual differences, for example, motivation and lack of physical fitness, which make stereotyping an impossibility. However, at the beginning it is best to train for three days in any week, normally Monday, Wednesday and Friday. This arrangement will give the beginner a chance to recover and recharge his or her batteries!

Still, if someone is exceptionally keen on the weight training aspect, the days off from lifting weights can be used to full advantage. For example, coaching films can be watched and technical drills can be practised without lifting any weights. It depends entirely on how motivated a person is to reach the top of his or her sport. Naturally if someone trains hard, a recovery period is essential, but the rest days can be used to supplement the training.

10 The supervisory role

Weight training is hard work and requires valuable time and effort to be organized properly, but it thrives best when efficiently supervised. Demonstrations and explanations of the technical factors must be professionally executed. All schedules and weight lifting record sheets must be kept up to date and arranged properly.

If a weight training programme is to be successful then the teacher or coach must be present to motivate and guide the participants to perform well. Groups should move simultaneously from one exercise to the next. The apparatus for each exercise should be prepared by the coach well in advance of the training session to save valuable time and to avoid delays caused by unforeseen problems. During the training period the coach or teacher should move around the performing area, offering advice and encouragement, particularly when things are not going well for the weight trainers. Remember that enthusiasm is contagious. If the coach or teacher is enthusiastic, everyone involved will also be so. Regular attendance on the part of both the participants and the coach or teacher is an important feature for a successful programme. The coach or teacher can be greatly helped by other qualified persons who can act as supervisors, enabling him or her to give more attention and time to individuals.

The weight training participant should be motivated through variations in the programme, competitions, and by having personal record sheets and improvement charts displayed on the walls of the performing area. A publicity campaign can be directed at the local press, radio and local sports centre. These and countless other jobs are a coach's and teacher's responsibility if a successful programme is to be achieved. The coach or teacher should decide well in advance how much effort is worth while to help participants in such a demanding physical activity.

11 Safety considerations

The sport of weight training can be dangerous if supervision is poor and the participants do not observe the codes of safety applicable to the sport. It is extremely important to maintain good discipline in the performing area and at no time should individuals train alone.

For a full review of the safety aspects of the sport see chapter 2, 'Safety factors in weight training' (pages 24–30).

Weight training for the handicapped

It is obvious that people can suffer from many types of handicaps or disabilities. The designation 'handicapped' includes the blind or partially sighted; the deaf; the cardiac; the physically disabled, including amputees, paraplegics; and the mentally handicapped. The degree or severity of disability will vary enormously among individuals, and because of this it can be appreciated that great difficulties are inherent when devising training or rehabilitation schedules. In the same way that schedules must be tailor-made to suit the individual requirement of able-bodied participants, so must they be for the handicapped.

Handicapped people expend great energy performing a relatively simple task, since the functional parts of their bodies have to compensate for those parts which have been reduced or lost. For example, people on crutches will use more energy and take longer to walk a given distance than an able-bodied person. They will therefore benefit from improving their general fitness, and weight training can be very useful in building up such qualities as strength, power, mobility, endurance, co-ordination; in turn self-confidence is increased.

Many handicapped people take part in sport competitively as is evident from the Paraplegic Games where competitors show themselves to possess great strength and stamina.

Weight training works for the handicapped for three basic reasons.

1   The applied resistance can be adjusted to suit the individual's level of strength and endurance at a given time and may be graduated so that the optimum weight can be achieved to ensure progressive muscular activity.

2   Many exercises exist which are suitable, perhaps modified in some cases, to allow any muscle group to be exercised.

3   It is possible to improve any component of fitness (strength, power, endurance) by employing different combinations of weights, repetitions and sets. As an example, if heavy weights are used and a low number of repetitions is performed, strength gains will be made, whilst using submaximal weights with a high number of repetitions will result in increased endurance.

The type of weight training exercises performed by a handicapped person will obviously depend upon his or her disability, the severity of the disability and the ratio between staff or spotters and those training at any one time during a session. Often handicapped participants require assistance in receiving a barbell or dumb-bell before commencing an exercise but again this depends on the nature and severity of the disability.

Taking these factors into account, many of the exercises described in this book may be performed with some modification. For example, the following exercises can be performed sitting down, and so they would be suitable for wheelchair participants.

1   Military press (figure 25)
2   Tricep stretch (figure 30)
3   Two arm curl (figure 28)
4   Upright rowing (figure 27)
5   Press behind neck (figure 24)
6   Lateral raise (figure 49)
7   Wrist curl (figure 34)
8   Reverse wrist curl (figure 35)
9   Forward raise (figure 36 and figure 51)
10   Reverse curl (figure 29)

With guidance, participants can be helped out of their wheelchairs on to a flat bench where they will be able to perform the following exercises in the same way as able-bodied trainers.

1   Bench press (figure 31)
2   Flyways (figure 52)
3   Straight arm pullover (figure 43)
4   Bent arm pullover (figure 44)

Handicapped people take part in a variety of sporting activities and many take advantage of weight training exercises to improve their performance. Some of the major sports in which, for example, people confined to a wheelchair participate are listed below with selected arm and shoulder exercises relevant to these sports. If the trainer's disability allows, leg exercises should also be practised to maintain overall fitness. The exercises are not given in any particular order, and sets or repetitions are not prescribed because, as we said earlier, schedules do have to be tailor-made for individual needs.

1 Archery

Weight training exercises
a   Upright rowing (figure 27)
b   Bench press (figure 31)
c   Tricep stretch (figure 30)
d   Military press (figure 25)
e   Wrist curl (figure 34)
f   Forward raise (figure 36 and figure 51)

2 Athletics (throwing events)

Weight training exercises
a   Bench press (figure 31)
b   Upright rowing (figure 27)
c   Tricep stretch (figure 30)
d   Military press (figure 25)
e   Straight arm pullover (figure 43)
f   Lateral raise (figure 49)

3 Basketball and netball

Weight training exercises
a Two arm curl (figure 28)
b Lateral raise (figure 49)
c Military press (figure 25)
d Straight arm pullover (figure 43)
e Tricep stretch (figure 30)
f Wrist curl (figure 34)

4 Swimming

Weight training exercises
a Bench press (figure 31)
b Lateral raise (figure 49)
c Military press (figure 25)
d Forward raise (figure 36 and figure 51)
e Tricep stretch (figure 30)
f Two arm curl (figure 28)

Weight training programmes for the handicapped can be divided into three main phases.

Phase one, or the initial phase, should concentrate on general conditioning, developing neuromuscular co-ordination and serving as an introduction to a schedule of exercises. The type and number of exercises performed in each schedule will need to be determined beforehand, but ideally two sets of about ten repetitions should be performed three times a week (for example, Monday, Wednesday, Friday).

The time taken on phase one will depend on numerous factors, and trainers should not move on to phase two until their therapists or other advisers are satisfied with the progress they are making.

Phase two should be designed primarily to develop strength, but the endurance fitness acquired in phase one should be maintained. A gradual and progressive increase in the weights used during the exercises is made with a decrease in the number of repetitions until the exercise can be performed comfortably six times with three sets. Training sessions should again be scheduled for three times a week, perhaps devoting Monday and Friday sessions to strength improvement and Wednesdays to endurance maintenance. Phase one should continue at all times with periodical variations in the exercises.

Handicapped people interested in taking part in sporting activities can progress on to phase three when the training schedule becomes much more specific and intense. Weight training schedules may then be practised four times a week.

Weight training, apart from helping to develop strength, power and mobility, can also be used to advantage in rehabilitation. It can prove invaluable for assisting the newly handicapped person's physical and psychological adjustment to, and victory over, disability, as well as providing opportunities for social integration. An increase in power and strength often gives a feeling of importance, prestige and success.

The sections on the values of the types of muscle contraction for rehabilitation purposes (page 7), the values of the group action of muscles (page 18), sport injuries (page 125), together with chapters 4 and 6, will provide further insight for the handicapped person to construct a sound exercise and weight training schedule.

4
Weight training exercises and terms

The various types of body movement are described in the section on 'Joint movement' (pages 7–12). Some weight training exercises involve one or more types of joint movement, depending on the nature of the exercise and the manner in which it is performed. There are literally hundreds of different exercises, some using weights and some not, and it would take a very long book to include all types of weight training exercises. In an attempt to be practical, we have included in this chapter many basic exercises to help the development of the entire body, with enough choice to plan a varied training schedule.

When selecting exercises one needs to consider several points. Firstly, ensure that the muscles which are desired to be developed are properly overloaded, that is, sufficient resistance is applied to a specific muscle group; secondly, decide whether a barbell or dumb-bell is best suited to a particular exercise; and finally, ensure that the exercise is simple and safe to execute. The simplicity of an exercise is important in the teaching situation, particularly for a large group when the training programme must be simple, safe and easy to administer. Difficult and complex exercises should be conducted in small groups with constant and expert supervision.

Basic lifting techniques

Lifting grips

There are a variety of grips used in weight training and it is important that the trainer has a firm and correct grip for a specific exercise. The various types of grip are as follows:

Overgrasp
The hands grip the bar with the palms facing the legs, and the bar between the fingers and thumb. The distance between the hands depends on the exercise being performed, but is generally just wider than shoulder-width apart.

Undergrasp
This is the opposite of the overgrasp grip in that the palms face away from the legs when gripping the bar, with the thumbs outermost and on top of the bar.

Alternate grasp
This is when one hand takes the position of the overgrasp and the other the undergrasp grip.

Hook grasp
This is a grip used mostly for heavy lifting. It is similar to the overgrasp grip except that the index finger of each hand is placed on the last digit or nail of the thumb. The hook grip helps to maintain a good hold on the bar when lifting great weights when immense gripping strength is required.

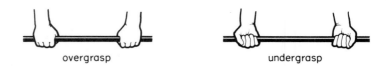

overgrasp   undergrasp

alternate grasp

Figure 10 The various grips

Lifting positions

Stance or feet positioning is very important in the execution of physical activities. This can be exemplified in all sports. A participant must be well-balanced to execute effective and powerful force.

Standing   The basic starting position for most weight training exercises is standing with the feet about shoulder-width apart and the toes pointing slightly outwards, the insteps directly under the bar. A comfortable position should be sought with the heels flat on the floor; the rest of the body remains erect with arms by the sides.

Crouch   This is another basic position used in weight training and required by many exercises in order to lift a barbell from the floor. From the standing position, bend from the hips

Figure 11 Standing position
Figure 12 Crouch position

and the knees to assume a crouch position and grip the bar with the hands slightly more than shoulder-width apart. The arms should be straight and outside the knees, back flat, head up and feet flat on the floor.

Thigh support For this position stand with the chest out and shoulders braced back, arms hanging so as to allow the bar to support or rest against the thighs. Any of the various grips may be used. It is often advisable to return the bar to the thigh support position having completed the number of repetitions required, before returning the bar to the floor. This provides for greater control of the exercise and the bar can be placed on the floor more lightly, thus preventing damage to the latter.

Chest rest This is another important position often assumed before commencing the counting of repetitions for an arm and shoulder exercise. It is sometimes referred to as the *clean* or *recurring* position. In the chest rest position the bar rests on the upper chest, with the elbows flexed and pointing forward to allow the bar to rest comfortably. The grip must be overgrasp, with the hands slightly more than shoulder-width apart. The legs should be straight and set shoulder-width apart with the trunk erect.

Figure 13 Thigh support
Figure 14 Chest rest

Shoulder rest Standing with feet astride, the barbell is held behind the neck with the bar resting across the shoulders and back of the neck. The shoulders should be braced back so that the bar is able to rest across the full width of the back and shoulders. An overgrasp grip is used with the hands slightly more than shoulder-width apart and the elbows flexed and pointing to the ground. To assume this position,

Figure 15 Shoulder rest

the bar may be lifted from the floor and pressed behind the neck or taken from a rack or frame already holding the barbell at shoulder level.

Prone   This position involves lying flat on the stomach with the arms by the sides of the body.

Supine   This position is the opposite of the prone position, and involves lying flat on the back, with the arms by the sides, looking up at the ceiling.

Weight training exercises

Weight training exercises can be divided into three broad categories: power, strength and general fitness and mobility exercises. Frequently power exercises are excluded from many sportsmen and sportswomen's training schedules but they are vital if improvement is to be made in sports involving dynamic or explosive actions. Power is a most desirable quality both for athletes and other sportspeople.

Power and strength will generally be developed from fast, rapid movements whilst slower movements will develop strength, and full range movements mobility. The manner in which an exercise is performed and the number of repetitions and sets carried out will depend on whether power, strength or mobility is required. Another factor to consider will be the choice of exercises in a given programme in relation to both the preceding exercise and the rest interval taken between the exercises.

No specific order has been given to the exercises described, but it is hoped that an adequate and varied schedule can be devised to suit individual needs. Always remember the weight training objectives, the nature of your own sport, and the time of year in relation to your competitive season when compiling a schedule.

Breathing technique

Correct breathing technique plays an important role in executing weight training exercises and must be practised if maximum effort is to be achieved. However, opinion seems to vary as to the best moment to inhale. Oxygen is a necessary component for muscular activity; therefore, to exert maximum effort during the pushing, pulling or lifting phase of an exercise inhalation needs to have taken place. It would be difficult to hold a strong position (that is with a heavy weight) with deflated lungs. We think that inhalation should be just prior to the most exerting phase of the exercise; for example, when pressing a barbell overhead from the chest, inhalation would be just prior to pressing the barbell and exhalation when the elbows lock or when the barbell is lowered to the chest from full extension of the arms. It is advisable to breathe during each repetition rather than to hold the breath for a given number of repetitions. Many exercises include two stages, one to lift the barbell to the starting position and one to execute the exercise itself for a given number of repetitions before returning the barbell to the floor. Correct breathing technique will play an important part in both stages of an exercise.

Exercises for power development

1 Dumb-bell jump squat

Body part exercised	Major muscles
Back extensors	Erector spinae
Hip extensors	Gluteus maximus
Knee extensors	Quadriceps
Plantarflexors of ankle	Gastrocnemius and soleus

Begin this exercise in the crouch position with the feet comfortably apart and a firm grip of each dumb-bell. With an explosive action, the legs and trunk extend to jump vertically so that the feet clear the floor. The object is to jump as high as possible. Care must be taken to land on the balls of the feet, bending the knees and hips on impact. Control of the dumb-bells during the exercise is achieved by holding them slightly away from the hips at arms length.

The dumb-bell jump squat is a vigorous and tiring exercise useful for many sports. Some athletes are known to hold a heavy barbell on their shoulders while doing jump squats. This may be suitable for the experienced lifter but jarring and injuries to the back can result, so great care is very important. Another variation of the dumb-bell jump squat is to have one foot slightly further forward than the other during the jumping phase, alternating for each repetition.

Figure 16 Dumb-bell jump squat

2 Power clean

Body part exercised	Major muscles
Plantarflexors of ankle	Gastrocnemius and soleus
Knee extensors	Quadriceps
Hip extensors	Gluteus maximus
Back extensors	Erector spinae
Elbow flexors	Brachialis and biceps
Shoulder abductors	Deltoid

Using the overgrasp grip, the barbell is lifted from the floor to the chest rest position in one continuous movement. The exercise is initiated by an explosive drive of the legs and hips until the legs are straight. The bar should have gained momentum and further upward lift of the barbell is gained by rising on the toes and pulling with the arms. The barbell should be kept close to the legs and body throughout the exercise. When the maximum pull or upward extension has been achieved, a rapid downward movement of the elbows is made to get the arms beneath the barbell and on to the chest. At the same time a slight bend of the knees is necessary to get under the bar and to place the barbell across the front of the chest. Having achieved this, one can then stand erect to assume the chest rest position remembering to force the elbows forwards, thus allowing the bar to rest on the chest and not to support the weight of the bar with the arms. To return the barbell to the floor, it should be lowered to the thigh support position first, and then to the floor to repeat the exercise.

The power clean is an important exercise for the athlete and is suited to most sportsmen and women. It is an excellent explosive exercise developing general body power, and if eight to ten repetitions of three sets are done, it will be found that the exercise is a good conditioner resulting in an increase in respiration for the lifter.

Figure 17 Power clean

3 The snatch

Body part exercised	Major muscles
Plantarflexors of ankle	Gastrocnemius and soleus
Knee extensors	Quadriceps
Hip extensors	Gluteus maximus
Back extensors	Erector spinae
Elbow extensors	Triceps
Shoulder abductors	Deltoid

The snatch is one of the two accepted Olympic lifts and may be performed in one of two ways. The aim is to lift the barbell from the floor to overhead with the arms straight, in one continuous movement; either the squat or split technique may be employed.

For the squat technique, assume the crouch position but with the feet slightly closer together and the hands placed wide apart with an overgrasp grip. The width of the grip is usually determined by measuring the distance from elbow

Figure 18 The snatch

to elbow when standing with the arms held out horizontally to the side, and the elbows flexed. With the lifter in the crouch position, the barbell is explosively driven upwards with the legs, keeping the barbell close to the legs and body, rising up on to the toes, extending maximally and elevating the shoulders. From this position pull on the barbell with the arms to get under it and at the same time jump both feet simultaneously to assume a wider stance so that the seat can fall between the heels. The toes should point outwards on landing and the feet should then be kept flat on the floor. Continue to press the barbell overhead while assuming a full squat position with the knees wide apart. Holding the barbell steady, the lifter can then extend the legs to stand erect, keeping the knees well apart and the barbell directly overhead.

With the split technique, the legs are split, one placed forward and the other behind the body, after maximum extension has been achieved. A deep split is needed with the rear leg resting on the toes, and the heel facing away from the body and the knee just clear of the floor. The leading leg should be almost fully flexed with the toes pointing slightly inwards. During the split phase the barbell is pressed overhead until the elbows lock. To assume the standing position, the front leg is straightened by sliding the foot backwards a short distance before sliding the rear foot forward until the feet are side by side about shoulder-width apart.

The snatch may be a difficult exercise to master but it is well worth the perseverence for it is an excellent exercise to develop power in the legs and arms. It calls for mobility in the hips and shoulders, and also the ankles if the squat technique is employed, since it is important for stability to keep the heels down flat on the floor when in the squat position. Remember that, regardless of the technique employed, the bar should be held in the overgrasp grip with the hands placed wide apart.

4 Clean and jerk

Body part exercised	Major muscles
Plantarflexors of ankle	Gastrocnemius and soleus
Knee extensors	Quadriceps
Hip extensors	Gluteus maximus
Back extensors	Erector spinae
Elbow flexors	Brachialis and biceps
Elbow extensors ⎫ jerk	Triceps
Shoulder abductors ⎬ phase	Deltoid

The clean and jerk constitutes the other Olympic lift along with the snatch. Assume the crouch position and lift the barbell to the chest in one continuous movement as described for the power clean. From the chest rest position, bend the knees about ten centimetres in a vertical dip, immediately drive vigorously upwards with the legs and jerk the barbell overhead until the elbows lock. Once the legs and ankles are fully extended, split the legs with a short and sharp movement. The split should not be as deep as it is for the snatch split, and the feet are slightly closer together with the hips remaining much higher. The heel of the rear leg remains off the floor. To return to the standing position, straighten the front leg slightly and slide it backwards, before stepping the rear foot forward in line with the front foot.

The clean and jerk is a good exercise for general development of the body and power for the arms and shoulders.

Figure 19 Clean and jerk

5 Power press

Body part exercised	Major muscles
Knee extensors	Quadriceps
Elbow extensors	Triceps
Shoulder abductors	Deltoid

This exercise is similar to the clean and jerk and is sometimes referred to as the *heave press*. Having cleaned the barbell to the chest rest position using an overgrasp grip, bend slightly from the hips and at the knees and then thrust the barbell vigorously from the chest to overhead by straightening the legs and pressing with the arms; the feet must remain motionless throughout the movement. Lower the barbell to the chest and repeat the exercise. To lower the barbell to the floor, bring it back into the chest rest position, on to the thighs and then on to the floor, keeping the back flat.

This is another excellent exercise for developing power in the arms and shoulders.

Figure 20 Power press

6 *Lunge and press*

Body part exercised	Major muscles
Knee extensors	Quadriceps
Hip extensors	Gluteus maximus
Elbow extensors	Triceps
Shoulder abductors	Deltoid

Clean the barbell to the chest rest position and place one foot forward to feel comfortable and balanced. Keeping the trunk upright step forward and dip the hips to assume what is referred to as the lunge position, with the leading knee directly in front of the forward foot, at the same time pressing the barbell vigorously above the head. To recover, press up with the leading leg and step backwards slightly, still keeping the barbell above the head. Once the feet have returned to the starting position, that is, one foot slightly in front of the other, lower the barbell on to the chest to repeat the exercise.

This exercise produces power in the arms and shoulders and mobility of the hips and knees. It can be done by alternating the forward leg and is a useful exercise for racket players and fencers.

Figure 21 Lunge and press

7 High pulls

Figure 22 High pulls

Body part exercised	Major muscles
Plantarflexors of ankle	Gastrocnemius and soleus
Knee extensors	Quadriceps
Hip extensors	Gluteus maximus
Back extensors	Erector spinae
Shoulder abductors	Deltoid

From the crouch position and using an overgrasp grip, drive hard with the legs and rise on to the toes in an attempt to pull the bar to the chin in one continuous movement. In the final position the legs should be fully extended with the arms out to the side and elbows flexed, and the wrists above the bar and flexed. Keeping the barbell under control lower it to the floor and repeat.

This exercise serves as a conditioner for fitness programmes and develops power in the legs and arms

8 Power curl

Body part exercised	Major muscles
Knee extensors	Quadriceps
Hip extensors	Gluteus maximus
Elbow flexors	Brachialis and biceps

Assume the crouch position using an undergrasp grip with the hands slightly more than shoulder-width apart. In one continuous movement, stand to an erect position and curl the barbell to the chest. Ensure that the back is flat throughout the exercise. Return the barbell in the same arc to the starting position and repeat. The exercise offers power development and co-ordination in the arms and legs.

Figure 23 Power curl

Exercises for strength
development
9 Press behind neck

Body part exercised	*Major muscles*
Elbow extensors	Triceps
Shoulder abductors	Deltoid

Lift the bar and place it in the shoulder rest position. The hands should be slightly more than shoulder-width apart and the feet parted sideways and flat on the floor. Press the

Figure 24 Press behind neck

barbell overhead until the elbows lock and then lower to repeat the exercise. Try to keep the head slightly forward to avoid contacting the back of it on lowering the bar! The movement develops shoulder mobility and exercises the smaller muscles around the scapulae. Breathe in on pressing the barbell and exhale on lowering.

10 Military press

Body part exercised	Major muscles
Elbow extensors	Triceps
Shoulder abductors	Deltoid

Clean the barbell to the chest rest position and place the feet about shoulder-width apart to feel comfortable. Press the barbell to full arm extension with the barbell directly overhead, keeping the knees straight and trunk upright throughout the press phase. Repeat as often as desired, before lowering the barbell to the chest, the thighs and then the floor, bending the knees and keeping the back flat in the latter phase of lowering.

Figure 25 Military press

11 Bent forward rowing

Body part exercised	Major muscles
Back extensors	Erector spinae
Elbow flexors	Brachialis and biceps
Shoulder retractors	Rhomboids

Stand with the feet slightly more than shoulder-width apart and bend forward from the hips so that the trunk is almost parallel to the floor. The head should be held in line with the trunk, the arms straight with an overgrasp grip on the bar and the hands more than shoulder-width apart. The knees should be slightly bent in order to keep the back flat throughout the whole movement and release tension in the lower back. Having assumed this position, pull the barbell strongly to the chest by bending the elbows and raising them sideways. Lower the barbell until the arms hang keeping the weighted discs just clear of the floor and then repeat the whole movement. Slight variations to this exercise can be made by pulling the barbell to different areas of the trunk, to the chest, abdomen and lower abdomen alternately.

Figure 26 Bent forward rowing

12 Upright rowing

Body part exercised	Major muscles
Shoulder abductors	Deltoid
Elbow flexors	Brachialis and biceps

Bend from the hips and knees and grip the barbell using an overgrasp grip with the hands about fifteen to twenty centimetres apart and the arms between the legs. Stand up so that the arms are hanging; then pull the barbell to the chin keeping the bar close to the body. Keep the elbows above the hands at all times. Lower the barbell to the thighs and repeat. If heavier weights are used the legs can assist the lifter by raising the heels just before the arm movement is completed; this is, however, a form of cheating for upright rowing.

Figure 27 Upright rowing

13 *Two arm curl*

Body part exercised	*Major muscles*
Elbow flexors	Brachialis and biceps

Using an undergrasp grip lift the barbell to the thigh support position. While keeping the upper arm motionless and close to the trunk, bend the elbows to curl the barbell to the chest and keep the trunk upright. Ensure that the elbows are kept still and against the side of the trunk to keep the resistance on the muscle group being exercised. If the elbows are forced forward and upward the resistance will be transferred away from the elbow flexors to the shoulder flexors. Several variations can be made to this exercise by altering the width of the grip, or by leaning forward, but keeping the back flat, so that greater resistance is offered when working in the inner range (see page 15).

Figure 28 Two arm curl

14 Reverse curl

Body part exercised	Major muscles
Elbow flexors	Brachialis and biceps
Wrist extensors	Extensor carpi muscles

With an overgrasp grip bring the barbell to the thigh support position. Keeping the upper arm motionless, curl the barbell to the chest so that the back of the hands nearly touch the shoulders. Return in the same arc and repeat. Less weight should be handled than in the two arm curl exercise since the wrist extensors are not as strong as the wrist flexors, and throughout the movement the barbell should be supported mainly on the thumbs.

Figure 29 Reverse curl

15 Tricep stretch

Body part exercised	Major muscles
Elbow extensors	Triceps

Clean and press the barbell with an overgrasp grip to position it behind the neck and shoulders. Carefully adjust the grip so that the hands are about shoulder-width apart ensuring that the elbows point directly forward; from this position press the barbell overhead by straightening the elbows. Lower the barbell to behind the head and repeat the movement.

Figure 30 Tricep stretch

16 Bench press

Body part exercised	Major muscles
Shoulder protractors (chest muscles)	Pectoralis major Deltoid (anterior fibres)
Elbow extensors	Triceps Serratus anterior

Figure 31 Bench press

The bench press requires the use of support stands or racks or the help of two people (spotters). Clear instructions must be given both to the spotters and the lifter as to when to take away the barbell on completion of the exercise. Having ascertained this, assume a supine position on a stable bench with the head, trunk and hips comfortably supported. The legs should straddle the bench with the feet flat on the floor either side of the bench.

Before taking the barbell from the racks or spotters, and using an overgrasp grip, position the hands an equal distance from the centre of the bar so that it will be balanced, and straighten the arms fully. The hands should be about shoulder-width apart although variations in grip width can be made. Lower the barbell under control to the chest and then press upwards to straighten the arms; this will constitute one repetition. The arms should be straight at both the beginning and end of the exercise and one should inhale on lowering the barbell to the chest and exhale as the arms straighten. If the elbows are pulled out sideways when lowering the barbell, the pectoral muscles will come into greater use. The bench press is usually a favourite among weight trainers and is a good exercise to develop power and strength of the chest and arms as well as being a good conditioner.

17 Inclined bench press

Body part exercised	*Major muscles*
Shoulder protractors (chest muscles)	Pectoralis major Deltoid (anterior fibres)
Elbow extensors	Triceps

This exercise is very similar to the bench press except that the bench is inclined. Lie on an inclined bench ensuring the feet are firmly on the floor or a block to prevent the body slipping downwards. Rest the bar in the chest rest position holding the barbell with an overgrasp grip, hands slightly more than shoulder-width apart. Press the barbell upwards to full arm extension, inhaling just prior to pressing and exhaling as the elbows lock. Lower the barbell to the chest and repeat. Once again it is advisable to have spotters to assist in this exercise.

Figure 32 Inclined bench press

18 Shoulder shrug

Body part exercised	*Major muscles*
Shoulder girdle elevators	Upper trapezius Levator scapulae Rhomboids

Take hold of the barbell using the overgrasp grip with the hands slightly more than shoulder-width apart. From the thigh support position, shrug the shoulders, bringing them as near to the ears as possible, and then lower them; the arms should remain straight throughout the whole movement.

Shoulder shrugging is a good exercise to mobilize the shoulder girdle, developing muscle definition of the upper trapezius and assisting in the development of other power exercises, such as the power clean. If relatively heavy weights are used, the exercise will also help to develop grip strength.

Figure 33 Shoulder shrug

19 Wrist curl

Body part exercised	*Major muscles*
Wrist flexors	Flexor carpi muscles

Hold the barbell using an undergrasp grip with the hands about shoulder-width apart, and sit on a bench with the back of the forearms only resting on the front of the thighs. The feet should be flat on the floor. Extend the wrist fully, allowing the barbell to roll as far as possible on the fingers. Keeping the forearms motionless curl the wrists to a maximum contraction by flexing the fingers and wrists. Under control, lower the barbell to the starting position and repeat.

Figure 34 Wrist curl

20 *Reverse wrist curl*

Body part exercised	Major muscles
Wrist extensors	Extensor carpi muscles

This is virtually the same as the wrist curl exercise except an overgrasp grip is employed. Allow the wrist to be fully flexed and then lift to extend the wrist maximally keeping the front of the forearms resting on the thighs. Return by gently lowering the hands to flex the wrists and repeat.

Figure 35 Reverse wrist curl

21 *Forward raise*

Body part exercised	Major muscles
Shoulder flexors	Deltoid (anterior fibres)
	Coracobrachialis
	Pectoralis major (clavicular portion)
Wrist extensors (static)	Extensor carpi muscles

Assume the thigh support position with an overgrasp grip and hands about shoulder-width apart. Keeping the trunk still and upright throughout, raise the barbell forward and upwards to overhead with the arms remaining straight at all times. Gently return the barbell through the same arc and then repeat. This exercise offers great resistance to the shoulder flexors due to the leverage obtained by keeping the arms straight. The same muscle groups work eccentrically when lowering the bar to the thigh support position. The exercise could be performed using an undergrasp grip, giving resistance to the wrist flexors instead of the wrist extensors.

Figure 36 Forward raise

22 Dead lift

Body part exercised	*Major muscles*
Knee extensors	Quadriceps
Hip extensors	Gluteus maximus
Back extensors	Erector spinae
Forearm (gripping)	Flexor and extensor carpi muscles

This exercise is usually performed with heavy weights but beginners should use a light weight until they become accustomed to the movements involved. Assume the crouch position using an alternate grasp grip on the bar. Ensure that the feet are comfortably apart and flat on the floor. Keeping the back flat at all times, attempt to straighten the legs to stand erect and to assume the thigh support position. The arms remain straight at all times. Gently, and under control, bend the knees and from the hips to lower the barbell to the floor and repeat. The dead lift is a good exercise to develop strength in the legs and back but ensure the back remains as flat as possible. Some lifters do a straight leg dead lift. We prefer to exclude this exercise, since the lower back has to be curved to pick up the barbell and this is not a strong stable position for the lower back. Furthermore, the exercise places great strain on the lower back and so it is more important to have the back flat and stable. If there is a need to do the straight leg dead lift, a much lighter weight should be used.

Figure 37 Dead lift

23 Back squat

Body part exercised	Major muscles
Knee extensors	Quadriceps
Hip extensors	Gluteus maximus
Back extensors	Erector spinae

Assume the shoulder rest position with the hands slightly more than shoulder-width apart. Ensure that the feet are comfortably apart and flat on the floor. If a relatively light weight is used, the barbell can be cleaned from the floor, and pressed behind the head. If a heavier weight is used as is the case in most instances, spotters, or racks, may be necessary.

From the shoulder rest position bend at the hips and knees to lower the trunk, breathing in at the same time. It is not advisable to go down further than when the thighs are parallel to the floor. Very rarely does any sportsperson need to thrust away from a full squat position. Having lowered sufficiently, drive hard upwards with the legs, exhaling at the same time, to resume the shoulder rest position. It is important to keep the shoulders braced back so that the bar lies against the full width of the shoulders and neck. Repeat as often as desired.

Every effort should be made to keep the heels down so that the feet are flat throughout the squatting phase thus providing a stable base. Some lifters raise their heels which calls for greater balance; to keep the heels down requires mobility in the ankles. If lifters lack this mobility they may, if they wish, support their heels on a block, but this is not ideal, and exercises to increase ankle mobility should be practised to avoid using a block.

The back squat is a basic exercise for many athletes and sportspeople since it offers good development of the lower limbs and is useful as a conditioner. It is therefore an important exercise to practise. Vary the exercise by jumping with both feet off the floor, resting the weight behind the shoulders. This is commonly known as the jump squat and should only be done by the competent weight trainer. For safety reasons, ensure that the knees bend slightly on landing.

Figure 38 Back squat

24 Front squat

Body part exercised	Major muscles
Knee extensors	Quadriceps
Hip extensors	Gluteus maximus
Back extensors	Erector spinae

Start this exercise in the chest rest position, using an overgrasp grip. The feet should be comfortably apart with the hands slightly more than shoulder-width apart. The exercise is much the same as the back squat where the hips and knees bend to lower the trunk and barbell until the thighs lie almost parallel to the floor. From this bent position drive vigorously upwards by straightening the hips and knees to resume the standing position. Repeat the exercise, inhaling on bending the legs and exhaling on straightening them.

Figure 39 Front squat

25 Calf raise

Body part exercised	*Major muscles*
Plantarflexors of ankle	Gastrocnemius and soleus

Figure 40 Calf raise

Place the barbell in the shoulder rest position by cleaning it to the chest first and then pressing it over to the back of the neck. If a heavy weight is required, since the calf muscles or plantarflexors are very strong, spotters or racks should be used. Stand with the feet about shoulder-width apart, and where possible have the toes on a firm block or discs so that they are higher than the heels. This will cause the ankle to dorsiflex and stretch the Achilles tendon, thus allowing for a greater range of movement in the ankles. From this balanced position raise the heels as high as possible keeping the toes motionless on the block, and then lower again under control to return. The exercise can be varied by pointing the toes outwards, inwards or straight; or by holding the barbell in the thigh support position using an overgrasp grip. The latter would involve holding the weight on the arms but would be useful in strengthening the grip.

26 Split squat

Body part exercised	Major muscles
Knee extensors	Quadriceps
Hip extensors	Gluteus maximus

Clean the barbell to the chest rest position using the overgrasp grip, then adjust the grip so that the hands are more than shoulder-width apart. Step well forward with one leg, checking that the toes of the rear foot point forward and the heel is slightly raised. Keep the bar high on the chest and ensure that the trunk is kept upright throughout. Once balanced, lower the body by bending the knees and from the hips, so that the weight of the barbell goes downwards and forwards until a low split position is achieved. In the split position, check that the knee of the front leg is ahead of the foot and the heel down. The rear heel should be off the ground and the toes pointing forward. The return is made by extending the leading leg until straight, ensuring that the trunk remains upright. On the last repetition recovery is made by straightening the leading leg and sliding the foot backwards slightly, then sliding the rear foot forward so that both feet are placed side by side and shoulder-width apart. Several variations to this exercise can be made by alternating the leading leg and lunging or stepping in different directions: forwards, diagonally or sideways. The split squat, with its variations, is an excellent exercise for racket players.

Figure 41 Split squat

27 Shoulder extension

Body part exercised	Major muscles
Shoulder extensors	Latissimus dorsi
	Pectoralis major (initial phases)
	Teres major
	Posterior deltoid
Elbow extensors	Triceps

The starting position for this exercise is rather different from others already described. Place the barbell on the floor and stand with the back to it. Bend the knees and hips, taking hold of the bar with an overgrasp grip, the hands about shoulder-width apart, and stand lifting the bar so that the arms hang straight. Ensure that the feet are comfortably apart, raise the barbell backwards and upwards as far as possible, keeping the arms straight and trunk erect. Lower gently to the back of the thighs and repeat. This is a good strengthening exercise for the shoulders and rear upper arm. A slight variation can be made to this exercise by leaning forward slightly with the knees flexed to assist in keeping the back flat. This allows for a greater range of movement to take place.

Figure 42 Shoulder extension

Exercises for mobility and general fitness
28 Straight arm pullover

Body part exercised	Major muscles
Shoulder extensors	Posterior deltoid
Thorax	Pectoralis major
	Teres major
	Latissimus dorsi
Elbow extensors	Triceps

Figure 43 Straight arm pullover

Lie supine on a bench to support the head, trunk and hips, straddling the bench with the feet placed flat on the floor. Hold the barbell over the chest with the arms straight and hands slightly more than shoulder-width apart. Gently lower the barbell a quarter of a circle or more breathing in at the same time. After a brief pause return the barbell in the same arc, exhaling at the same time. It is advisable to warm-up the muscles of the thorax and shoulders by stretching before commencing the exercise and to do the first two or three repetitions steadily, not taking the barbell too low. Concentrate on the correct breathing technique, so as to gain full benefit from the exercise. The straight arm pullover is a useful exercise for javelin throwers and tennis serving.

29 Bent arm pullover

Body part exercised	*Major muscles*
Shoulder extensors	Posterior deltoid
Thorax	Pectoralis major
	Teres major
	Latissimus dorsi
Elbow extensors	Triceps

Assume a supine position on a bench with the feet straddled either side and the head supported as near to the end of the bench as possible. Place the barbell on the floor at the head of the bench. Reach out and with the overgrasp grip take hold of the bar lifting it to rest on the chest. Trying to keep the elbows at right-angles throughout, raise the barbell up over the head and lower, keeping it just clear of the floor. Inhale while doing this. Return the barbell in the same arc and exhale.

Figure 44 Bent arm pullover

30 Split clean

Body part exercised	Major muscles
Plantarflexors of ankle	Gastrocnemius and soleus
Knee extensors	Quadriceps
Hip extensors	Gluteus maximus
Back extensors	Erector spinae
Elbow flexors	Brachialis and biceps

Assume the crouch position with an overgrasp grip and hands placed slightly more than shoulder-width apart. Drive vigorously with the legs until maximum extension is achieved and the toes just clear the floor. Then immediately split the feet rapidly, attempting to place them in a fore and aft stance with the body going downward and forward, but keeping the trunk upright. A deep split should be achieved so that the knee of the front leg is in front of the leading foot. The heel of the rear foot should be well up with the knee just clear of the floor, and the toes pointing forward.

As the feet are split, the lifter should pull on the barbell to bring the elbows beneath it, supporting it on the chest. To recover, push with the front leg and bring it backwards slightly, then bring the rear foot in line with the front foot, still keeping the barbell on the chest. Lower the barbell to the thigh support position, then to the floor and repeat.

A relatively light weight should be used initially, since the exercise calls for control and co-ordination. Heavier weights can be used at a later stage and this particular movement is an alternative method to the power clean of cleaning the bar to the chest and is sometimes used in preparation for the clean and jerk. The split clean is a dynamic exercise and causes stretching of the knee extensors of the leading leg and hip flexors of the rear leg. The exercise can be varied by alternating the front leg.

Figure 45 Split clean

31 Split snatch balance press

Body part exercised	Major muscles
Knee extensors	Quadriceps
Hip extensors	Gluteus maximus
Shoulder abductors	Deltoid
Elbow extensors	Triceps

Clean the barbell to the chest rest position using an overgrasp grip. Place the hands wide apart and step one leg well forward with the heel of the rear foot raised, toes pointing forward. Keeping the feet stationary, dip the body to assume a deep split position with the legs and at the same time press the barbell upwards and forwards with the arms into the overhead position. The trunk should remain motionless throughout. Check that the knee of the front leg is in front of the leading ankle and that the front foot is flat. The rear heel should be well clear of the floor with the toes pointing forward. To recover, extend the front leg and lower the barbell to the chest and repeat. Change the leading leg alternately or after a set number of repetitions. The exercise provides power and mobility for the shoulders and mobility of the hips and knees.

Figure 46 Split snatch balance press

32 Squat snatch balance press

Body part exercised	Major muscles
Shoulder abductors	Deltoid
Elbow extensors	Triceps
Knee extensors	Quadriceps
Hip extensors	Gluteus maximus

Start this exercise from the shoulder rest position with an overgrasp grip and hands wide apart, as described in the snatch exercise (page 56); the feet should be slightly more than shoulder-width apart and should remain flat throughout the movement with the toes pointing outwards at an angle of forty-five degrees. Once firmly balanced, dip gently with a slight bend from the hips and knees, before immediately driving upwards with the legs and pressing hard with the arms to take the barbell overhead. Once the legs have driven upwards, bend the hips and knees again to drop under the barbell into a full squat with the seat between the ankles and knees pointing outwards. The arms should continue to press until the elbows lock. To recover, extend both the hips and knees, keeping the knees pointing outwards and trunk upright, and barbell held overhead. Lower the barbell into the shoulder rest position and repeat the movement. This exercise helps to increase power in the arms and legs and improves mobility in the shoulders, hips and knees.

Figure 47 Squat snatch balance press

33 Side split squat

Body part exercised	Major muscles
Knee extensors	Quadriceps
Hip extensors	Gluteus maximus
Hip adductors	Adductor magnus and longus

Figure 48 Side split squat

Assume the shoulder rest position, with the feet wide apart. Keeping the trunk upright throughout, gently bend the right knee and move the body and barbell to the right, if possible keeping the heel flat on the floor. In this position the muscles on the inside of the left thigh (adductors) will be stretched. To recover, extend the right knee and move the body to the left so that both legs are straight. Repeat the movement to the left and to the right. The exercise is a useful one to develop hip abduction mobility and to stretch the hip adductors. Racket players may find this exercise useful when stretching to play low return shots.

Exercising with dumb-bells

The use of dumb-bells can offer variation to the training schedule, thus eliminating the onset of boredom. Dumb-bells can be used to develop certain muscle groups, mobilize certain joints or serve for general fitness when used in circuit training programmes. Dumb-bells are limited to the arms and trunk although they can be strapped to the foot, but special iron boots designed for this purpose are then needed. A great range of dumb-bell exercises can be devised, but it is not possible to list them all. The exercises described should offer variety, and involve the development of many muscle groups.

34 Lateral raise

Body part exercised	Major muscles
Shoulder abductors	Supraspinatus Deltoid

Figure 49 Lateral raise

Stand with the feet apart holding the dumb-bells by the thighs at arms length and with the palms of the hands facing the body. Keeping the knuckles uppermost, raise the arms to the side to the level of the top of the head. Hold this position momentarily before lowering under control and then repeat. Breathe in before raising the arms and exhale when lowering. This exercise can be done sitting on a bench as an alternative method and variation.

35 Bent forward lateral raise

Figure 50 Bent forward lateral raise

Body part exercised	Major muscles
Shoulder retractors	Rhomboids
	Latissimus dorsi
	Teres major
Elbow extensors (static)	Triceps

Stand with feet comfortably apart and lean well forward, with the knees slightly flexed and back flat, and maintain this position throughout the exercise. Hold the dumb-bells allowing the arms to hang. Raise the dumb-bells sideways as high as possible, maintaining straight arms with knuckles uppermost. Gently lower in the same arc and repeat. Breathe in before raising and out when lowering the arms.

36 Forward raise

Body part exercised	Major muscles
Shoulder flexors	Anterior deltoid
	Coracobrachialis
	Pectoralis major
	(clavicular portion)
Wrist extensors (static)	Extensor carpi muscles

Take up a position with the body upright, and the dumb-bells resting on front of the thighs with the palms of the hands facing the body. Raise the dumb-bells forward until they are in line with the eyes, keeping the arms straight and knuckles uppermost. Hold momentarily and lower under control to the starting position. Breathe in when raising the dumb-bells and out when lowering them. A variation can be made to this exercise by holding the dumb-bells in an undergrasp grip or by sitting on a bench using either grip.

Figure 51 Forward raise

37 Lateral raise, supine (flyways)

Body part exercised	*Major muscles*
Shoulder protractors	Subscapularis
	Anterior deltoid
	Pectoralis major
	Coracobrachialis

Lie supine on a bench with feet placed firmly flat on the floor. Hold the dumb-bells directly over the chest with the arms straight. Keeping the arms straight throughout the whole movement, lower them sideways to just below shoulder level and return. Use a light weight initially for this exercise and if tightness occurs at the elbows or shoulders, bend the elbows very slightly. Breathe in when lowering the dumb-bells and exhale on the return. This is a good exercise for the thorax which is stretched, as well as for the shoulders, and is often practised by discus throwers.

Figure 52 Lateral raise, supine (flyways)

38 Dumb-bell side bend

Figure 53 Dumb-bell side
bend

Body part exercised	Major muscles
Trunk flexors	Obliques
	Sacrospinalis

Standing erect, with the feet apart, take hold of a dumb-bell in one hand and place the other hand behind the head with the elbow pointing sideways. Keeping the body square at all times, bend from the waist and lean to the dumb-bell side as far as possible. Return to the upright position and repeat. Change hands after a certain number of repetitions to exercise the other side of the body. Breathe in when bending sideways and out to stand erect.

39 Dumb-bell press

Body part exercised	Major muscles
Shoulder abductors	Deltoid
Elbow extensors	Triceps

Stand erect with feet comfortably apart. Hold the dumb-bells in front of the shoulders, with the arms bent at the elbows. Press the dumb-bells overhead, keeping the body erect and knees straight throughout. Check that the elbows lock. Lower under control to the shoulders and repeat. This exercise can be varied by doing alternate arm pressing: as one arm presses the other lowers.

Figure 54 Dumb-bell press

40 Bent forward single arm rowing

Body part exercised	Major muscles
Shoulder retractors	Posterior deltoid Latissimus dorsi Teres major

The exercise commences in a bent forward position with the feet comfortably apart, the left hand placed just above the left knee, and the right hand grasping the dumb-bell. From this position, pull and lift the dumb-bell vigorously along the side of the body, rotating the trunk slightly, to finish with the dumb-bell just above the right shoulder. The right wrist should remain above the dumb-bell at all times, and the left hand should not move from just above the left knee. Return to the starting position with the dumb-bell just clear of the floor and repeat, before changing hands. Slight variations to this exercise can be made by supporting the free hand on a low bench and by limiting the rotation of the trunk on lifting so that a truer rowing action is achieved.

Figure 55 Bent forward single arm rowing

41 Single arm tricep stretch

Body part exercised	Major muscles
Elbow extensors	Triceps

Stand erect with the feet comfortably apart. Hold the dumb-bell behind the neck with the right hand and place the left hand on the left hip. Straighten the right elbow vigorously until the dumb-bell is above the head. Lower and repeat the exercise, before changing hands.

Figure 56 Single arm tricep stretch

42 *Dumb-bell screw curl*

Body part exercised	*Major muscles*
Elbow flexors	Brachioradialis and brachialis
Forearm supinators	Biceps Supinator

Stand erect, holding the dumb-bells at the side of the thighs with the arms straight, palms facing inwards, and the feet comfortably apart. Bend the elbows strongly to bring the hands just in front of the shoulders, and about midway through this arc, twist the forearms so that the palms face the head. Gently lower in the same arc, untwisting the forearm, then repeat.

Figure 57 Dumb-bell screw curl

5
Weight training programmes for selected sports

Today many coaches and teachers are using weight training techniques to help to condition and strengthen their sportsmen and sportswomen, but there are still some who are unfamiliar with the basic scientific principles behind, and methods of, resistance exercise programmes. The programmes in this chapter are presented so that everyone involved in sport, beginner or ambitious athlete, can realise the many advantages of weight training programmes.

Archery

Two keys to a good performance in the sport of archery are undoubtedly muscle steadiness and consistency in duplicating each step of the shooting action. Shakiness during the draw or when one reaches the anchor point (the point on the side of the head where the pulling arm rests at full draw) is usually due to muscle weakness, particularly in the arms, shoulders and upper back. Weight training exercises can help to strengthen the muscles in these parts of the body.

Table 8 Programme for archery

Order of exercise	Type of exercise	Sets	Reps	Kilogrammes Men	Women	Development area of body	Figure
1	Warm-up	(schedule as described earlier)					—
2	Bench press	3	10	25	12½	Upper chest/arms	31
3	Bent forward rowing	3	10	15	7½	Front of upper arms	26
4	Wrist curl	3	10	7½	2½	Forearms/wrists	34
5	Military press	3	10	20	10	Shoulders	25
6	Tricep stretch	3	10	15	5½	Back of upper arms	30
7	Sit-ups	3	15	No weight		Abdominals	—

Athletics

After many years experience of successful coaching and competing in track and field athletics, during which time various programmes of weight training were used, we would suggest the following exercises as being suitable for participants in the jumping, throwing and running events.

However, before listing specific weight training programmes, we should first mention flexibility of the joints which is of such importance to all athletes. Flexibility in the joints is essential if athletes are to perform at a high level and as a result coaches and teachers must include exercises for flexibility in their training programmes.

There are numerous flexibility exercises, for example, the hurdle stretch, hurdle stretch on the ground, touching the toes with legs straight and trunk rotation movements.

During the weight training programme, a majority of coaches and teachers suggest that an emphasis should be put on those muscles which are used in the athlete's own event. This is extremely important. As an example, it is of little value to a shot putter to concentrate entirely on looking good by developing those bicep muscles by performing the two arm curl all day and night! The shot putter should be exercising those muscles that propel the shot a long way, namely the shoulders and legs, practising for example the bench press and squat.

So that no weaknesses occur it is imperative that the training session should incorporate all-round physical development. Athletes should work on their weak points as well as their strong ones. For example, the coach or teacher should encourage the athlete who dislikes the squat routine to perform this exercise at the start of the session, otherwise it will be left until the next day!

Beyond this, variations may be made in the training schedules suggested according to an individual's preferences and requirements, but it is recommended that a young athlete, who has never practised weight training before, should submit his or her schedule to a qualified weight training coach for approval in case many changes are needed!

Programmes for athletics

Table 9 The sprints

Order of exercise	Type of exercise	Sets	Reps	Kilogrammes		Development area of body	Figure
				Men	Women		
1	Warm-up	(schedule as described earlier)					—
2	Press behind neck	3	10	15	7½	Upper shoulders	24
3	Split squat	3	8	30	15	Legs	41
4	Bench press	3	10	25	12½	Upper chest/arms	31
5	Sit-ups	3	15	No weight		Abdominals	—
6	Back squat	3	10	25	12½	Legs	38
7	Straight arm pullover	3	10	10	5	Chest/arms	43
8	Calf raise	3	10	20	10	Lower legs	40

Table 10 The hurdles

Order of exercise	Type of exercise	Sets	Reps	Kilogrammes Men	Women	Development area of body	Figure
1	Warm-up		(schedule as described earlier)				—
2	Jump squat	3	10	20	10	Legs	16
3	Straight arm pullover	3	10	10	5	Chest/arms	43
4	Snatch	3	8	25	12½	Arms/legs	18
5	Calf raise	3	10	20	10	Lower legs	40
6	Sit-ups	3	15	No weight		Abdominals	—

Table 11 High jump

Order of exercise	Type of exercise	Sets	Reps	Kilogrammes Men	Women	Development area of body	Figure
1	Warm-up		(schedule as described earlier)				—
2	Jump squat	3	10	20	10	Legs	16
3	Straight arm pullover	3	10	10	5	Chest/arms	43
4	Sit-ups	3	15	No weight		Abdominals	—
5	Back squat	3	10	25	12½	Legs	38
6	Side bend	3	10	10	5	Trunk	53
7	Calf raise	3	10	20	10	Lower legs	40

Table 12 Javelin

Order of exercise	Type of exercise	Sets	Reps	Kilogrammes Men	Women	Development area of body	Figure
1	Warm-up		(schedule as described earlier)				—
2	Tricep stretch	3	10	15	5	Upper arms	30
3	Side bend	3	10	10	5	Trunk	53
4	Bench press	3	10	25	12½	Upper chest/arms	31
5	Front squat	3	10	20	10	Legs	39
6	Snatch	3	8	25	12½	Arms/legs	18
7	Sit-ups	3	15	No weight		Abdominals	—

Table 13 Discus

Order of exercise	Type of exercise	Sets	Reps	Kilogrammes		Development area of body	Figure
				Men	Women		
1	Warm-up		(schedule as described earlier)				—
2	Back squat	3	10	25	12½	Legs	38
3	Bench press	3	10	25	12½	Upper chest/ arms	31
4	Front squat	3	10	20	10	Legs	39
5	Flyways	3	8	7½	2½	Arms/shoulders	52
6	Lateral raise	3	8	10	2½	Shoulders	49
7	Side bend	3	10	10	5	Trunk	53
8	Sit-ups	3	15	No weight		Abdominals	—

Table 14 Hammer

Order of exercise	Type of exercise	Sets	Reps	Kilogrammes	Development area of body	Figure
				Men		
1	Warm-up		(schedule as described earlier)			—
2	Shoulder shrug	3	8	20	Shoulders	33
3	Power clean	3	6	30	Legs	17
4	Bench press	3	10	25	Upper chest/ arms	31
5	Dead lift	4	6	45	Legs/back	37
6	Sit-ups	3	15	No weight	Abdominals	—
7	High pulls	3	8	35	Shoulders	22

Badminton

All badminton players must be extremely physically fit and agile, but, as far as possible, the training must be organized to suit the individual because each one has his or her own strengths and weaknesses. In badminton, physical fitness means the ability to undergo the longest periods of physical and mental stress during a competition, and the ability to recover quickly after a brief resting period, so that badminton skills are not impaired.

Many times during the closing stages of a competition it is the fitter player who succeeds in the end even when skill is equal. When stamina wanes, so does skill. Today's game is so competitive that physical fitness is essential and just as important as technique and tactical play. Physical fitness embraces stamina, strength, speed, power, mobility and skill. These factors can be attained by a combination of running, weight training, circuit training and speed and reaction games.

Table 15 Programme for badminton

Order of exercise	Type of exercise	Sets	Reps	Kilogrammes Men	Women	Development area of body	Figure
1	Warm-up		(schedule as described earlier)				—
2	Press behind neck	3	10	15	7½	Upper shoulders	24
3	Sit-ups	3	15	No weight		Abdominals	—
4	Curls	3	10	12½	5	Upper arms	28
5	Back squat	3	10	25	12½	Legs	38
6	Bench press	3	10	25	12½	Upper chest/arms	31
7	Bent arm pullover	3	10	15	7½	Chest/arms	44
8	Lateral raise	3	8	5	2½	Shoulders	49
9	Side bend	3	10	10	5	Trunk	53

Baseball

Baseball players must be able to perform the skills of the game extremely quickly and accurately. In addition, power in throwing and batting is imperative, and speed is important in fielding and base running. However, baseball does not require tremendous amounts of muscular or cardiovascular endurance.

Key muscle groups in baseball include the forearms, deltoids and upper back, but as with most sports, virtually all of the body's skeletal muscles come into play.

It is important during the competitive season that weight training exercises are performed only during the early days of each week, so that they will not have a detrimental effect on timing and co-ordination on game days, which are normally scheduled for weekends.

Table 16 Programme for baseball

Order of exercise	Type of exercise	Sets	Reps	Kilogrammes Men	Development area of body	Figure
1	Warm-up		(schedule as described earlier)			—
2	Power clean	3	6	30	Legs	17
3	Bench press	3	10	25	Upper chest/arms	31
4	Lateral raise	3	8	10	Shoulders	49
5	Wrist curl	3	10	7½	Forearms/wrists	34
6	Press behind neck	3	10	15	Upper shoulder	24
7	Tricep stretch	3	10	15	Upper arms	30
8	Sit-ups	3	15	No weight	Abdominals	—

Basketball

Undoubtedly every basketball coach and teacher is mainly interested in results and recognises the tangential values that may be obtained from competition. As a result the coach and teacher is at all times considering factors which may help to produce excellent performances. Executing techniques perfectly, employing tactics, developing team spirit, practising healthy habits and building strength and endurance are all important.

But most probably, the least thought-out factor will be that of building strength and endurance, even though they are of great importance to successful participation, adding co-ordination and helping to improve techniques as well as increasing speed.

In order to develop the appropriate muscles a programme of resistance exercises, carefully planned on a basis of overload, is of paramount importance. Only recently have some basketball coaches recognized the importance of building strength and endurance and only a handful utilize information which is easily obtainable for practical coaching purposes from the British Amateur Weight Lifting Association. Although the procedures are simple they need regular and persistent application in order to achieve the desired result.

Strength is important in basketball both for jumping and shooting and also endurance is an essential requirement, in order to last a full game at a high competitive level. A coach or teacher may not have a 208 centimetre post player, but he or she may compensate for this lack of height by building strength in the legs of the players to enable them to achieve great heights in jumping. As much as twenty centimetres has been added to a player's vertical jump as a result of increasing the strength of the leg muscles by weight training. It is quite possible for relatively small players (175 cm) to increase their jump so that they can dunk the ball with both hands.

If a player is to be able to shoot with accuracy throughout a game, additional strength is needed in the finger and arm muscles (biceps brachii and the triceps). Players who have strong arms and fingers can normally expect to shoot the one hand set shot with consistent accuracy. Once again, weight training can be employed to develop this extra strength.

A common ailment in basketball is that of sore shins (shin splints) which are often sustained by both novices and experienced but out of condition players; they can be most painful and incapacitating. However, if strength is built up in the muscles of the lower leg, this annoying injury may be eliminated entirely or very quickly.

Stronger muscles are able to withstand better the enormous amount of pounding to which the legs are subjected in basketball.

The exercises which can be employed are substantial and varied. The following, however, are a typical selection and have been used by successful basketball coaches and teachers.

Table 17 Programme for basketball

Order of exercise	Type of exercise	Sets	Reps	Kilogrammes Men	Kilogrammes Women	Development area of body	Figure
1	Warm-up		(schedule as described earlier)				—
2	Side bend	3	10	10	5	Trunk	53
3	Alternate dumb-bell press	3	10	10	5	Arms	54
4	Jump squat	3	10	20	10	Legs	16
5	Straight arm pullover	3	10	10	5	Chest/arms	43
6	Calf raise	3	10	20	10	Lower legs	40
7	Tricep stretch	3	10	15	5	Backs of upper arms	30
8	Back squat	3	10	25	12½	Legs	38

Boxing

Boxing is one sport which requires that the participant is in peak physical condition at the time of a contest. It is therefore essential that the training programme covers the wide range of qualities which come under the classifications of fitness. Mobility, speed, power, endurance, and a high degree of skill are the major physical components required for success in boxing.

Table 18 Programme for boxing

Order of exercise	Type of exercise	Sets	Reps	Kilogrammes Men	Development area of body	Figure
1	Warm-up		(schedule as described earlier)			—
2	Bench press	3	10	25	Upper chest/arms	31
3	Jump squat	3	10	20	Legs	16
4	Curls	3	10	12½	Upper arms	28
5	Press behind neck	3	10	15	Upper shoulder	24
6	Alternate dumb-bell press	3	10	10	Arms	54
7	Sit-ups	3	15	No weight	Abdominals	—

To punch effectively the boxer needs a wide range of body movements especially at the hip and shoulder joints. These can be attained by a careful mobility schedule. The boxer also requires power, and this is where the application of weight training will prove useful to him. Pure strength is of little use, but strength combined with speed can be a vital factor in the make-up of the top-class boxer. Power (force times velocity) can be built up with a careful weight training schedule. Such a schedule is outlined on page 92.

Cricket

In the modern game of cricket, with emphasis increasingly on limited overs, it is imperative that players are extremely fit and alert. The three qualities essential to the cricketer today, namely skill, stamina and speed, depend to a large extent on physical fitness. Weight training can undoubtedly help to achieve this, particularly the stamina and speed aspects. With competitions becoming fiercer and more frequent, it is advisable that cricketers, both men and women, incorporate weight training sessions in their training build-up.

Table 19 Programme for cricket

Order of exercise	Type of exercise	Sets	Reps	Kilogrammes		Development area of body	Figure
				Men	Women		
1	Warm-up		(schedule as described earlier)				—
2	Lateral raise	3	8	5	2½	Shoulders	49
3	Press behind neck	3	10	15	7½	Upper shoulders	24
4	Back squat	3	10	25	12½	Legs	38
5	Straight arm pullover	3	10	10	5	Chest/arms	43
6	Tricep stretch	3	10	15	5	Upper arms	30
7	Calf raise	3	10	20	10	Lower legs	40
8	Sit-ups	3	15	No weight		Abdominals	—

Football (USA)

Virtually every football player uses weights in his training schedule to improve strength and power, because, of course, high levels of these are needed for this extremely physical and demanding sport.

The skills of blocking, tackling, running, passing, and kicking can be improved enormously through weight training and body conditioning. For example, both blocking and tackling skills require a swift burst of power (strength and speed). Therefore, if strength is increased, each can be improved accordingly.

During the off-season it is advisable that football players condition themselves by practising a variety of physical activities such as basketball, swimming and jogging. These activities should be supplemented with weight training sessions designed to maintain a high level of muscular strength and endurance. The weight training programme should exercise all of the major muscle groups, but with concentration on the leg extensors, back extensors and the arm and shoulder muscles.

During the competitive season the players should be in perfect physical condition and it is imperative that the players practise weight training in order to maintain their strength and power to a high level. A deterioration of strength and power will obviously have an adverse effect on the players' condition, both mentally and physically.

A weight training programme for American footballers is outlined below.

Table 20 Programme for football (USA)

Order of exercise	Type of exercise	Sets	Reps	Kilogrammes Men	Development area of body	Figure
1	Warm-up			(schedule as described earlier)		—
2	Bench press	3	10	25	Upper chest/ arms	31
3	Back squat	3	10	25	Legs	38
4	Military press	3	10	20	Shoulders	25
5	Power clean	3	6	30	Legs	17
6	Shoulder shrug	3	8	20	Shoulders	33
7	Dead lift	4	6	45	Legs/back	37
8	Sit-ups	3	15	No weight	Abdominals	—

Golf

This is one sport where a small person has a wonderful opportunity to excel if he or she possesses powerful wrists and shoulders. Gary Player, for example, is a golfer who is relatively small in stature but has managed to stay at the top of his profession for many years. It is not surprising, therefore, that one hears that he practises weight training to offset his handicap in size.

A golfer must have strong wrists and shoulders because the distance a golf ball may be hit depends primarily on timing and wrist and shoulder strength. When the club head hits the ball, the swing must be so perfectly executed that the full power of the body is against the ball. The final impetus is given by the hands, and it is through them that all the power and force of the arms, shoulders and the remainder of the body is transferred. It is important therefore that the golfer should aim to develop the arms and to some extent the trunk region, to gain full advantage of the swing. Several exercises exist to strengthen the hands, wrists and forearms, and a suggested programme for the beginner is outlined below.

Table 21 Programme for golf

Order of exercise	Type of exercise	Sets	Reps	Kilogrammes Men	Women	Development area of body	Figure
1	Warm-up		(schedule as described earlier)				—
2	Lateral raise	3	8	5	2½	Shoulders	49
3	Power clean	3	6	30	15	Legs	17
4	Wrist curl	3	10	7½	2½	Forearms/wrists	34
5	Sit-ups	3	15	No weight		Abdominals	—
6	Reverse wrist curl	3	12	7½	2½	Forearms/wrists	35
7	Hyper-extensions of the back	3	15	No weight		Back	—

Gymnastics

All gymnastic activities require precision performances which rely heavily upon high levels of strength and skill. As a result, a large part of the gymnast's formal training programme should emphasize the development of these abilities. Muscular endurance in the upper part of the body is also extremely important, but this is for the most part a by-product of strength or it is developed at the same time as strength. A reasonable level of cardiovascular endurance is also required of the gymnast in addition to an unusual amount of flexibility in certain regions of the body.

Table 22 Programme for gymnastics

Order of exercise	Type of exercise	Sets	Reps	Kilogrammes Men	Women	Development area of body	Figure
1	Warm-up		(schedule as described earlier)				—
2	Bench press	3	10	25	12½	Upper chest/ arms	31
3	Back squat	3	10	25	12½	Legs	38
4	Lateral raise	3	8	5	2½	Shoulders	49
5	Sit-ups	3	15	No weight		Abdominals	—
6	Press behind neck	3	10	20	10	Shoulders	24
7	Power clean	3	6	30	15	Legs	17

It takes many years for the gymnast to develop the strength required to perform certain routines. The desired levels of muscle strength are usually obtained through weight training activities, but the weight training programme designed for this purpose should be supplemented with a well-rounded mobility and stretching session.

Hockey

To reach a high standard of playing, today's hockey player must be extremely fit, particularly during tournaments. He or she must be able to retain mastery of the important technical facets of the game even when fatigued and, above all, execute skillful movements accurately and with speed. The technical facets include such skills as passing, stopping, scoring and dribbling. To achieve this mastery, the modern hockey player must be physically fit, yet at the same time mobile.

As in most sports, fitness for hockey means long, painful and continuous training sessions. The human body has to be well prepared to endure continuous running, often under pressure, for many minutes, while expending additional energy on producing the skills of the game.

Weight training can contribute enormously to the achievement of peak fitness and general muscular endurance for the modern hockey player.

Table 23 Programme for hockey

Order of exercise	Type of exercise	Sets	Reps	Kilogrammes		Development area of body	Figure
				Men	Women		
1	Warm-up	(schedule as described earlier)					—
2	Reverse wrist curl	3	12	7½	2½	Forearms/wrists	35
3	Jump squat	3	10	10	5	Legs	16
4	Wrist curl	3	10	7½	2½	Forearms/wrists	34
5	Lateral raise	3	8	10	2½	Shoulders	49
6	Split squat	4	8	30	15	Legs	41
7	High pulls	3	8	35	17½	Shoulders	22
8	Sit-ups	3	15	No weight		Abdominals	—

Lacrosse

As in hockey, general physical fitness of the highest degree is required in lacrosse. The game requires that the players have great endurance and the ability to take some punishing body contact.

Again weight training can help the lacrosse player to achieve peak physical fitness. In addition, strength gains can be obtained by following a carefully prescribed schedule, thereby enabling the lacrosse player to compete strongly, especially in hard physical matches.

Table 24 Programme for lacrosse

Order of exercise	Type of exercise	Sets	Reps	Kilogrammes Men	Kilogrammes Women	Development area of body	Figure
1	Warm-up		(schedule as described earlier)				—
2	Power clean	3	6	30	15	Legs	17
3	Back squat	3	10	25	12½	Legs	38
4	Military press	3	10	20	10	Shoulders	25
5	Reverse wrist curl	3	12	7½	2½	Forearms/wrists	35
6	Tricep stretch	3	10	15	5	Back of upper arms	30
7	Wrist curl	3	10	7½	2½	Forearms/wrists	34
8	Sit-ups	3	15	No weight		Abdominals	—

Netball

Many basic skills in netball, such as running, jumping, ball manipulation, getting free from opponents, marking and intercepting a pass, are common to other games. The game of netball also requires that players have good footwork. They must be ready to move quickly in any direction, jump higher than the opponents to receive the ball and, on landing, remain balanced.

Weight training can help enormously to achieve this athletic ability.

Table 25 Programme for netball

Order of exercise	Type of exercise	Sets	Reps	Kilogrammes Women	Development area of body	Figure
1	Warm-up		(schedule as described earlier)			—
2	Jump squat	3	10	10	Legs	16
3	Lateral raise	3	8	2½	Arms/chest	49
4	Side bends	3	10	5	Trunk	53
5	Side split squat	3	10	10	Legs	48
6	Tricep stretch	3	10	5	Back of upper arms	30
7	Sit-ups	3	15	No weight	Abdominals	—

Rowing

Apart from mastery of the techniques of rowing there are four main physical qualities which the coach or teacher should aim to develop in his or her training squad. These qualities are strength, endurance, speed and speed-endurance respectively.

Strength and endurance are developed during the preparation period of training, that is, during the winter months. The development of strength is achieved by weight training and endurance by circuit training and long distance rowing in the water, as well as by low rate full pressure paddling in the boat or by small boat training. If boredom becomes prevalent activities like jogging and squash will help the rower to keep in shape and maintain his or her endurance capabilities.

During the competitive season (summer) the accent should be directed to developing speed and speed-endurance. Failure to secure these essential qualities will often result in defeat for the rower.

Exercises for the development of the strength needed for rowing are outlined below in the suggested programme for rowing.

Table 26 Programme for rowing

Order of exercise	Type of exercise	Sets	Reps	Kilogrammes		Development area of body	Figure
				Men	Women		
1	Warm-up	(schedule as described earlier)					—
2	Curls	3	10	12½	5	Upper arms	28
3	Press behind neck	3	10	15	7½	Upper shoulders	24
4	Back squat	3	10	25	12½	Legs	38
5	High pulls	3	18	35	17½	Shoulders	22
6	Sit-ups	3	15	No weight		Abdominals	—
7	Bench press	3	10	25	12½	Upper chest/ arms	31
8	Bent forward rowing	3	10	15	7½	Front of upper arms	26
9	Dead lift	4	6	45	22½	Legs/back	37

Rugby

Although the different positions in rugby tend to require a different emphasis on the fundamental characteristics of the players, there are some characteristics which tend to be common to all good rugby players. These include high levels of strength and power, agility, quick reactions and speed of acceleration.

It is recommended that rugby players condition themselves during the off-season with a variety of vigorous activities such as basketball, swimming, squash and jogging. Activities of this nature should be supplemented with a weight training programme designed to maintain a high level of muscular strength and endurance. The programme should exercise all the major muscle groups, but place emphasis on the knee extensors (the quadriceps), the back extensors and the muscles of the arms and shoulders.

Once the competitive season arrives, the programme should be aimed at maintaining the weight levels of lifting rather than trying to improve strength with heavier weights.

A typical programme for beginners or out-of-condition rugby players is shown below.

Table 27 Programme for rugby

Order of exercise	Type of exercise	Sets	Reps	Kilogrammes Men	Kilogrammes Women	Development area of body	Figure
1	Warm-up	(schedule as described earlier)					—
2	Back squat	3	10	25	12½	Legs	38
3	Bench press	3	10	25	12½	Upper chest/ arms	31
4	High pulls	3	8	35	17½	Shoulders	22
5	Sit-ups	3	15	No weight		Abdominals	—
6	Power press	3	10	25	12½	Shoulders	20
7	Dead lift	4	6	45	22½	Legs/back	37

Soccer

Considerable research in the field of sport science has improved the efficiency of training methods. These scientific results have highlighted the fact that soccer coaches and clubs need to implement these methods if their players are to compete successfully at the highest level. One of these methods is weight training, which develops muscular strength and endurance. Consequently, many soccer clubs today encourage their players to participate in this physical activity to improve their overall fitness.

The soccer player must be fit, agile, fast and powerful. As we mentioned earlier in the book, there is only one way to gain strength and power and that is by progressive resistance exercises. The weight training programme must be well supervised with all-round body strength the main objective. Strength training could be included as part of a whole fitness training session, and, if this is done, it should be performed at the end of the session, otherwise interference with soccer skills might take place.

However, as in all sports, it is important to remember that there are five principles of training which will serve as a useful guide to the coach or teacher when considering the training programme. The five principles are overload, measurement and evaluation, specificity, competition and variety of activity.

Weight training exercises which are suitable for the development of power as it is applied in soccer are shown below in the programme for soccer.

Table 28 Programme for soccer

| Order of exercise | Type of exercise | Sets | Reps | Kilogrammes | | Development area of body | Figure |
				Men	Women		
1	Warm-up		(schedule as described earlier)				—
2	Military press	3	10	20	10	Shoulders	25
3	Jump squat	3	10	10	5	Legs	16
4	Sit-ups	3	15	No weight		Abdominals	—
5	Calf raise	3	10	20	10	Lower legs	40
6	Power clean	3	6	30	15	Legs	17

Squash

Squash is a game which is gaining rapidly in popularity, even though it is a physically demanding sport. To make progress in squash one must be aware of the importance of the tactical, technical and physical aspects. Development

Table 29 Programme for squash

| Order of exercise | Type of exercise | Sets | Reps | Kilogrammes | | Development area of body | Figure |
				Men	Women		
1	Warm-up		(schedule as described earlier)				—
2	Press behind neck	3	10	15	7½	Upper shoulders	24
3	Wrist curl	3	10	7½	2½	Forearms/wrists	34
4	Side bend	3	10	10	5	Trunk	53
5	Jump squat	3	10	10	5	Legs	16
6	Lateral raise	3	8	5	2½	Shoulders	49
7	Split squat	4	8	30	15	Legs	41
8	Sit-ups	3	15	No weight		Abdominals	—

of the physical aspect involves making sure that one is fit enough to stand up to all the demands of a highly competitive and lengthy match.

The same principles that pertain to the game of badminton apply to squash.

Swimming

The primary purpose of weight training is to increase the overall strength of selected muscle groups. Although most swimming coaches and teachers agree that competitive swimmers must have powerful muscles, there is much disagreement as to how this power should be acquired. The majority agree that weight training will increase power but a small percentage contend that the increase will be accompanied by shortened muscles and restricted action of the joints. However, recent research evidence has proved that this is not the case and that flexibility is enhanced.

Swimming alone will not develop the muscular strength that is required for individuals to attain their maximum performance, because water resistance is a constant factor, therefore overloading is difficult. As a result, strength should be built by the much harder resistances that can be found in weight training. A programme for all swimmers is included below.

Table 30 Programme for swimming

Order of exercise	Type of exercise	Sets	Reps	Kilogrammes		Development area of body	Figure
				Men	Women		
1	Warm-up	(schedule as described earlier)					—
2	Sit-ups	3	15	No weight		Abdominals	—
3	Back squat	3	10	25	12½	Legs	38
4	Tricep stretch	3	10	15	5	Back of upper arms	30
5	Lateral raise	3	8	5	2½	Arms/chest	49
6	Dead lift	4	6	45	22½	Lower back/legs	37
7	Bench press	3	10	25	12½	Upper chest/ arms	31

Tennis

Tennis has become a game which is played all the year round. As a result of fierce competition, top-class matches can last several hours, thereby forcing players of this calibre to be in excellent physical condition to compete successfully.

A light weight training programme, along with endurance running, is beneficial for keeping the total muscular system well-conditioned. However, strenuous endurance and weight training activities should be avoided during the three days prior to a competition to allow a sufficient recovery period.

Table 31 Programme for tennis

Order of exercise	Type of exercise	Sets	Reps	Kilogrammes Men	Kilogrammes Women	Development area of body	Figure
1	Warm-up		(schedule as described earlier)				—
2	Military press	3	10	20	10	Shoulders	25
3	Side bend	3	10	20	5	Trunk	53
4	Wrist curl	3	10	7½	2½	Forearms/wrists	34
5	Back squat	3	10	25	12½	Legs	38
6	Straight arm pullover	3	10	10	5	Chest/arms	43
7	Snatch	3	8	25	12½	Arms/legs	18
8	Sit-ups	3	15	No weight		Abdominals	—

Volleyball

The game of volleyball has progressed from being a simple physical activity of moving the ball back and forth across the net. Today's game requires that the volleyball player is skilful and has a great deal of endurance. All the players in the team must be fit, because the game is unique in that each participant plays every position in rotation. This requires the players to be in good physical condition and skilled in all positions of play.

Weight training will most certainly help today's volleyball players to become more powerful and fitter. A guide to suitable exercises with particular emphasis on leg work is shown below.

Table 32 Programme for volleyball

Order of exercise	Type of exercise	Sets	Reps	Kilogrammes Men	Kilogrammes Women	Development area of body	Figure
1	Warm-up		(schedule as described earlier)				—
2	Jump squat	3	10	20	10	Legs	16
3	Side bends	3	10	10	5	Trunk	53
4	Military press	3	10	20	10	Shoulders	25
5	Back squat	3	10	25	12½	Legs	38
6	Wrist curl	3	10	7½	2½	Forearms/wrists	34
7	Calf raise	3	10	20	10	Lower legs	40
8	Sit-ups	3	15	No weight		Abdominals	—

Wrestling

Success in wrestling is dependent primarily upon strength, agility and endurance in addition to knowledge of correct technique. If a participant is strong and agile, it is most probable that he or she can develop into a top wrestler.

Wrestlers must have an abundance of endurance to be able to compete at a high rate of performance throughout a contest. Related to agility are reaction time and speed of movement, which are also extremely important.

It goes without saying that the wrestler should train with weights to develop strength and endurance. However, it must be recognized that, because wrestlers vary enormously in ability and physical fitness, they cannot all follow the same training programme. A suggested weight training programme for the wrestler is shown below.

Table 33 Programme for wrestling

Order of exercise	Type of exercise	Sets	Reps	Kilogrammes Men	Kilogrammes Women	Development area of body	Figure
1	Warm-up		(schedule as described earlier)				—
2	Curls	3	10	12½	5	Upper arms	28
3	High pulls	3	8	35	17½	Shoulders	22
4	Back squat	3	10	25	12½	Legs	38
5	Bench press	3	10	25	12½	Upper chest/ arms	31
6	Dead lift	4	6	45	22½	Legs/back	37
7	Sit-ups	3	15	No weight		Abdominals	—

Conclusion

Training with weights has become recognized, particularly of late, as one of the best methods of training for sport. Numerous champions have given credit to weight training for the improvement in their performances.

Undoubtedly progressive resistance exercises develop the physique, strengthen muscles, improve stamina and give a feeling of well-being.

Experience and research have both shown that a high level of strength is essential in all sports if excellence is to be achieved and, in some sports, strength is of paramount importance. Top honours do not always go to the strongest and fastest competitors, but on most occasions they do.

6
The multigym and other strength training methods

A variety of mechanical aids has been devised in recent years to meet the increasing pursuit of health and fitness. Gymnasia and other exercise areas are gradually losing popularity to the rapidly emerging health clubs, as emphasis is placed on individual fitness and health. The multigym or multi-station unit has become a popular piece of apparatus for strength training and caters for the health conscious individual and the Olympic athlete.

The multigym

Multigyms are designed in a simple compact form to provide a wide range of exercises for different parts of the body where space is minimal. They differ greatly to incorporate a variety of exercises which may be done simultaneously by a group of people and some multigym units have eighteen or more exercise stations. There are also many varied single unit exercise stations, some of which may allow several exercises to be done (see figure 58).

Figure 58 The multigym. Army School of Physical Training Instructors demonstrating that multigym exercises can be performed in a confined space to gain physical fitness. (By kind permission of Power Sports International Ltd)

Different types of multigyms provide facilities for a great number of exercises, dependent, to a certain extent, on the number of exercise stations they contain; possible exercises include the bench press, leg press, high and low pulleys, shoulder press, sit-ups, back extensions, chinning bar, wrist and neck conditioners, rowing, hip flexion, knee extension, knee flexion and tricep dips. These and many other exercises can be done with varying resistance levels.

Use of the multigym is spreading throughout the world and innumerable organizations, such as large businesses, sports and health clubs, military establishments, rehabilitation units, fire and police training centres, sport centres, prison services and educational institutions, have such a facility.

These multigyms have certain inherent advantages over other conventional training devices. They are a great space saving device yet are able to cater for several participants at once. They are portable and require little or no fixing. Storage poses no problems and they are very safe to use. Above all, they are fun to use and provide a wide variety of exercises.

Strength training principles

Coaches and sport scientists are always seeking better and more efficient training methods for gaining strength and power in the hope of improving sporting performances. Advocates of the multigym and other similar training machines claim that these have greater advantages for strength gains than conventional weight training. Firstly, let us consider briefly and without too much detailed scientific analysis, the mechanics involved in weight training so that comparisons can be drawn.

Most weight training and callisthenic (stretching) exercises are examples of the *constant resistance* mode of training or *isotonics*. The latter, as stated in chapter 1 (page 7), refers to 'equal tone or tension', implying that a constant level of muscle tension exists throughout a given range of movement. In fact, only the resistance of the weight (barbell or dumb-bell), the body and gravity remains constant. There is considerable alteration in muscle tension during a typical dynamic concentric muscle contraction due to the continually changing angles of the muscle attachments.

Ideally, each repetition of an exercise should be performed against a maximum resistance. This, however, would prevent a step by step progression before fatigue or exhaustion follows. In practice, the weight or resistance can be set no higher than the lifter's estimated maximum strength, which is at the weakest joint position in the range of movement and during the final repetition. Thus, it is only the last repetition of each set which can cause local muscular exhaustion or failure. A major limitation, therefore, of constant resistance training is that the lifter works with a submaximal weight during all but the final repetition of each set. Failure only results at one point in the total range of movement, that is, the weakest point.

Since the advent of the multigym, such terms as *dynamic* and *automatic variable resistance* have become an extension to a coach's vocabulary. Nissen's Universal Centurian System incorporates dynamic variable resistance and Powersport International incorporates the automatic variable resistance method. These two terms seem to be synonymous and the latter will be used for our purposes.

Many training machines use levers, cams, hydraulic systems and other mechanical arrangements to provide variable resistance throughout varying ranges of movement. Briefly, this means that the resistance is automatically increased at those points where the muscles are strongest and is decreased where the muscles are weakest, hence the term variable resistance. (See section on the angle of pull of a muscle, page 112.)

Advocates of such machines claim that a greater training effect is experienced over a wider range of movement, in that more resistance is offered to muscles throughout a greater range. Variable resistance training has, however, only two main physiological advantages over the constant resistance form of training: it seems to offer uniform resistance to the muscles throughout the entire range of movement, and it tries to overcome the tendency for failure to occur only at the weakest point in the range of movement. Most modern training machines have successfully achieved these physiological advantages, although it must be pointed out that no variable resistance machine can match the exact shapes of the resistance and strength levels throughout a given range for all participants.

The similarity of variable and constant resistance training is that, in each case, an increase in applied force causes an increase in movement velocity. This means that speed of movement is not controlled and movement or limb accelerations are possible. Furthermore, the only true maximum contraction will be the last repetition of a set that is carried to exhaustion or failure. By definition, velocity is the rate of movement in a particular direction and acceleration is the rate of change in velocity.

Isokinetic training

Some exercise machines incorporate the principles of iso-kinetics. This term means 'equal motion' and generally refers to a type of dynamic exercise or action in which the movement velocity remains constant. Some doubt exists as to whether the term isokinetics refers to constant angular or linear velocity, for a uniform rate of rotary limb movement is not accompanied by a uniform rate of linear muscular shortening. In this respect, the term *accommodating resistance* is preferred. Isokinetic equipment offers accommodating resistance by providing a resistance force which varies automatically so that it is continuously equal and opposite to any applied muscular force. To put it another way, isokinetic machines provide resistance that accommodates to the force applied to it. The machine resists with exactly the same force that the participant applies, and, as a result, regulates the speed of the muscle contraction.

Since no weights are used in this type of machine, training velocities may approach or exceed actual sporting performances. Movement velocities are held constant throughout a specified range of movement, thus there can be no limb acceleration when a true accommodating resistance machine is used. That is, regardless of the force or strength exerted (beyond a minimal amount), the resistance or force will exactly balance (accommodate) the muscular force that is applied. Therefore, there can be no net force remaining and, according to Newton's first law, no acceleration. This lack of limb acceleration is thus a limiting factor of accommodating resistance training.

Newton's first law is also known as the *law of inertia*. Inertia is an inherent property by which a body resists a change in movement. If a body or object is at rest, its inertia will tend to keep it at rest; and, if in motion, its inertia will tend to keep it in motion. It is necessary to exert a force on an object to accelerate it because of the object's property of inertia.

In spite of a lack of acceleration, accommodating resistance training is of great value in improving general conditioning. A limb velocity which approximates to that used in a sport can be pre-set enabling the participant to exert maximum velocity force at each point throughout the entire range of movement on each repetition. The major feature of this type of machine is that it accommodates, or automatically adjusts, to the participant's changing strength at various joint angles or limb positions throughout all the repetitions of an entire exercise set.

If near maximum force is applied when using such machines, more work can be done per unit of time with accommodating resistance training than with any other available form of training. It is generally thought that muscles can work more thoroughly when training with accommodating resistance, so time is used more effectively and good results are obtained in less time. The evidence of some research studies according to Pipes and Wilmore (1975, 1976) suggests that accommodating resistance exercise is perhaps the most effective method of training for improved strength and transfer to sports performance if conducted rapidly. These authors also say that most athletes and coaches report muscle soreness is virtually non-existent following accommodating resistance training.

To conclude, accommodating resistance implies a resistant force which continuously equals any applied muscular force. That is, no matter how much strength is applied, there will be no acceleration. Limb velocity will remain fixed at a pre-determined value. The participant can then exert maximum force, at a desired velocity, over the full range of movement in each repetition.

Clearly, most types of exercise machines do not meet the accommodating resistance objectives. Many rely on pulley and weight stacks to provide constant resistance, whilst others include levers, cams, hydraulic systems and other compensating mechanisms to provide variable resistance.

Figure 59 The single station exerciser
This station provides a compact progressive resistance unit offering up to 30 classic resistance exercises. It is ideal for children, ladies, beginners or Olympic sportsmen and sportswomen.
(By kind permission of Power Sports International Ltd)

Equipping a sports hall

When contemplating equipping a gymnasium or sports hall with a multigym and single exercise units, there are several points to consider. The range of equipment available is both comprehensive and varied. Many manufacturers offer the same basic machines but often with different emphases and they are usually accompanied by excellent wall charts depicting a variety of exercises. Many machines are themselves multi-purpose, designed to exercise a variety of muscle groups. Single or multi-purpose equipment is available from many major manufacturers to meet individual requirements and specifications.

Several points must be carefully considered when purchasing gymnasium equipment, including:

1 Is the equipment easy to assemble and store?
2 Is it free standing, or does it require bolting to the floor?
3 Is a special floor surface required?
4 What purpose will the equipment serve?
5 Will the equipment accommodate all levels of user needs?
6 Is the equipment easy to use and adjust?

Isometric training

In isometric training, muscular force is usually exerted against a fixed object so there is no movement of either the object or the body segment involved. It is generally thought that isometric training increases strength. Contractions of six seconds at two thirds maximum is often quoted as a way of obtaining maximum strength gains, but the evidence supporting such a claim remains inconclusive and unsubstantiated. Doubt exists on how many contractions are necessary and the degree of contraction needed to obtain maximum strength gains.

If strength gains do occur with isometric exercises, an assumption can be made in that they would only be specific to the joint angle used during training. An increase, for example, in elbow flexion strength with the joint at ninety degrees would not necessarily ensure strength gains at angles of sixty or a hundred and twenty degrees. Hence, if increased strength is required throughout a given movement, isometric exercises should be performed at several joint angles or positions in the range of movement.

Another issue currently under debate is whether isometric training reduces flexibility. Since most sporting activities involve bodily movements of varying degrees, extremes of ranges of movement may be neglected unless a conscious effort is made to this effect. An isometric training session should, therefore, include mobility exercises, preferably before and after the main training schedule.

A major drawback with isometric training is that the participant may not be putting enough effort into the contraction, but merely goes through the motions. There is no immediate goal and only the most conscientious person would derive the full benefits.

We do not advocate the use of isometric training as the sole method of training since it does not have the advantage of exercising the full range of movement. It may be a useful addition on occasions to add variety, to break monotony or to avoid staleness.

Angle of pull

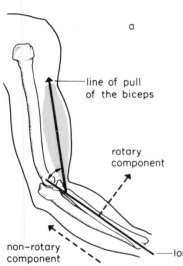

Other types of machines and apparatus used for exercising incorporate the principles of pulleys and springs. The principle of levers was discussed in chapter 1 (page 19). There are several types of training apparatus but only pulleys and springs will be discussed here. Before this, however, the concept of a muscle's angle of pull must be grasped.

Besides the effect of the relative length of the body levers, due to the varying lengths of bones, the action of a muscle is modified by the direction in which it pulls on the lever. The angle between a muscle's line of pull and the long axis of the bony lever to which it is inserted is known as the angle of pull. The axis is a straight line between the mid-points of both ends of the bone. This can be seen more clearly in figure 60.

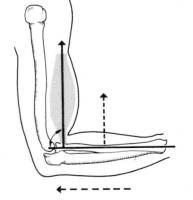

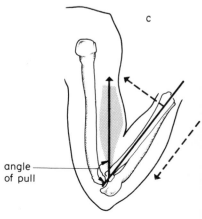

Figure 60 The line of pull of the biceps muscle at various angles

The pull which gives the greatest mechanical advantage is that of the right angle because no part of the force is wasted, since all the force goes to move the lever in the desired direction. If, however, the angle of pull is other than ninety degrees, the force is divided into two components; the first is a rotary component which causes the lever to turn, and the other a non-rotary component which pulls in the direction of the joint being moved. These two are at right angles to each other.

At angles of less than ninety degrees, part of the muscular pull acts to pull the bone lengthwise (non-rotary component) into the joint, thereby increasing the friction of the joint and reducing the amount of pull available to perform the movement. In the case of the biceps acting on the elbow in figure 60a, the joint is slightly flexed at about forty-five degrees. The non-rotary component helps to stabilize the joint, for it has a tendency to pull the long lever (forearm) towards the elbow joint. Thus, in angles of pull less than ninety degrees, the non-rotary component has a stabilizing effect on the joint.

When a muscle's angle of pull is greater than ninety degrees, the non-rotary component tends to pull the bony lever away from the joint producing a dislocating effect which reduces the stability of the joint (figure 60c). This occurs only rarely when a muscle has contracted to its limit of shortening, by which time little force is left.

Figure 60b depicts the biceps' angle of pull at ninety degrees, this being the optimal angle of pull for any muscle, since the entire force of the muscle is acting to rotate the bony lever around its axis (elbow joint).

A muscle's angle of pull will change with every degree of joint movement. The size of the angle has a direct bearing on the effectiveness of the muscle's pull in moving the bony lever. The angle of pull of most muscles in the resting state is less than ninety degrees. This means that the non-rotary component of force is directed into the joint, giving it stability.

A knowledge and understanding of the angle of pull of specific muscles can hold certain values. For instance, it is desirable in some activities or movements for a person to begin a movement when the joint is at right angles. Many young adults, or sportsmen or women may be unable or too weak through injury to perform, for example, a chin to the bar (that is, hanging from a beam at arms length and then pulling with the arms to bring the chin to the beam) unless they start at a ninety degree angle at the elbow joint. It would be easier to start in this position because of the more advantageous angle of pull. The application of this theory can compensate for a lack of sufficient strength and may be used to advantage for those beginning weight training or conditioning exercises. Furthermore, it can be very useful for rehabilitation purposes.

Pulleys

A pulley is a small grooved wheel which readily rotates about an axis passing through the centre and at right angles to it. The axis is supported by a framework or block, and a cord or wire is passed along the groove of the pulley with a weight on one end. It will be necessary to apply an equal force to the other end to prevent it falling. The weight and power of the two ends acting in opposite directions cause a strain on the cord referred to as 'tension in the cord'.

Pulleys provide a means of changing the direction of a force so that the force is applied at a different angle, thus achieving a more effective force in a given movement than would otherwise be possible. There are three main types of pulley systems: a single fixed pulley, a single movable pulley and a pulley combining the first two. The single fixed pulley is the only type which is represented in the human body and serves two purposes. It will either change the direction of a force to give a muscle a greater angle of pull, or it will change the direction of a force to produce an entirely different movement than it would otherwise perform.

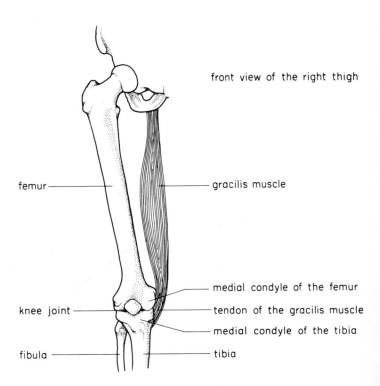

front view of the right thigh

femur

gracilis muscle

medial condyle of the femur

knee joint

tendon of the gracilis muscle

medial condyle of the tibia

fibula

tibia

Figure 61 The gracilis muscle showing its pulley action, giving it a greater angle of pull.

There are several examples in the body which resemble the principle of the single fixed pulley. For example, the angle of pull of the gracilis muscle (the most medial muscle of the thigh) tendon is increased by the shape of the medial condyles of the femur and tibia bones around the knee. The tendon passes over the condyles and is inserted into the tibia. Its main action is to flex the knee and assist adduction of the hip. This example is illustrated in figure 61.

Many multigyms and exercise machines contain pulleys to enable certain exercises to be performed; for example, the 'lat machine' provides a facility to exercise the latissimus dorsi muscle, and perform rowing exercises and bicep curls. The main purpose of pulleys, therefore, is to change the direction of a force but not its magnitude acting on the pulley cord.

Springs

The elasticity property of an object enables it to regain or resume its original form after it has been stretched or distorted by the application of a force. The force acting on the object and causing the distortion is called *stress* and the extent of change in size or shape is called *strain*.

Hooke's law states that the strain is proportional to the stress producing it. However, this only applies so long as the strain is not too great, for once the so-called 'elastic limit' is surpassed, permanent deformation results. Thus, Hooke's law is only applicable until the elastic limit is reached.

A spring consists of a uniform coil of wire which is extensible and which may be used to resist or assist the force of a muscular contraction. It can be extended or elongated by fixing one end of the spring and applying a force to the other end and in the direction of its long axis. The increase in length of a spring is directly proportional to the magnitude of the force applied in stretching it. Springs are often used as an aid to exercise, a prime example being the 'chest expander'.

The weight of a spring

Standard springs are graded according to the weight which must be applied to stretch them to a predetermined length. This is the force necessary to stretch the spring to its maximum. A tape is inserted within the coils of the spring and it becomes taut when the maximum pull is reached. The tape will also serve to prevent the spring from being overstretched and causing consequent damage to it. The material and thickness of the wire and the diameter of its coils will determine the weight of the spring.

115

Springs may be used to resist movement, assist movement (when the recoil of the spring is used) and as oscillators. When an applied force, used to stretch a spring, is removed the spring returns to its original length. The potential energy stored in the spring during extension is released as kinetic energy causing the recoil. If a weight is attached to a vertical spring and raised, then immediately released, an oscillatory movement is produced by the spring, the amplitude of which decreases gradually until the spring comes to rest in equilibrium.

Two or more springs may be used together and arranged either in *parallel* (side by side) or in *series* (end to end forming one long spring). The force required to stretch both springs in parallel to their maximum will be the sum of the strengths of each individual spring. If two springs of ten kilogrammes and fifteen kilogrammes are in parallel, the net force will be twenty-five kilogrammes, having the effect of one twenty-five kilogramme spring.

The weight of two equal springs in series will be the same as for just one of the springs. However, the amount by which they must be extended in order to reach the limit of extension is double that required for a single spring.

7
Additional considerations for the improvement of human performance

There are a large number of factors which affect human performance, some of which may favour certain individuals whilst adversely affecting others. Collectively referred to as *ergogenic aids* (anything which may be considered to elevate performance) these factors can broadly be classified into two categories, special foods and diets and various phenomena: for example, warm-up, music, hypnosis, mental rehearsal, information feedback and hot and cold applications. Each of these phenomena is a very detailed subject and it would be beyond the scope of this book to analyse them, or the other substances which may increase performance.

The study of human performance is a very complex task. Some factors may suit certain individuals, depending upon the level of their exposure to them, whilst others may react unfavourably towards them. The problems or challenges that confront coaches, sportsmen and sportswomen prompt them to become conversant with the many aids available and to decide which of these may be advantageous, and at what level or degree they should be incorporated. To assist this task, the 'personality type' and motivation levels of each individual must be studied, in that each person is unique. All factors which may be seen to increase human performance are closely integrated, but the problem will always be in determining which have the most beneficial effect on an individual and what level of exposure is needed.

1 The effects of nutrition on physical activity

Man has always sought various means to improve his physical capacity. Diet has been thought to be an important factor and athletes and scientists have tried and tested the values of various nutritional substances. The general consensus drawn by researchers reviewing the relationship between nutritional intake and physical performance is that a well-balanced diet is all that is necessary to produce optimum performance. Sportsmen and women and their coaches are not, however, convinced and continue to manipulate their diet, seeking ways to enhance their performances.

Psychological effects

Some individuals are affected psychologically by their diet and physical capacity. Many people, particularly athletes, are generally convinced that certain food products are necessary to reach peak performance. For example, during the 1960s many track athletes frequently consumed honey and/or tea prior to competing. The tea may have reduced the onset of dehydration and ionic imbalance and the honey may have served to elevate blood sugar levels. The efficacy of such practice remains uncertain, but the essential factor is that if an athlete is convinced that a certain food supplement is necessary for successful performance, then in all probability that nutrient is a necessary component for that particular individual.

Foodstuffs Various foodstuffs have been used and studied regarding their value to aid performance, including proteins, fats and carbohydrates. Proteins are chemical compounds made up in varying proportions of nitrogen, carbon, hydrogen and oxygen. Cheese, fish, meat and beans are very rich in proteins. They are essential substances for muscles, skin, internal organs and other soft tissues of the body. It is known that proteins are not a significant fuel for physical activity although there is some support for the idea that a greater protein intake can increase the production of muscle in weight lifters, wrestlers and field event specialists. However, most of the protein is simply broken down, its nitrogen is lost in the urine and sweat, and the remainder of its components is converted to fat. The general consensus among researchers is that little, if any, additional benefits are gained beyond those already found in a well-balanced diet.

Fats are chiefly derived from animal sources such as milk, butter, eggs and cheese. They serve several functions in the body, such as acting as a source of energy, as a store for an energy reserve and they provide certain vitamins essential for health and growth.

Carbohydrates are made up of varying proportions of carbon, hydrogen and oxygen, the latter two being in the same proportion as they are in water, 2:1. Bread, cereals, rice, potatoes and sugar are sources of carbohydrates. Sugar of a slightly different kind is also available from fruit (fructose) and milk (lactose). Carbohydrates are substances which are readily convertible into energy, and when digested they very quickly become the same substance, glucose. All carbohydrates must be converted into glucose before they can be utilized in the body.

A diet high in fats and carbohydrates has frequently been followed by many athletes as a means of increasing physical performance. However, this will depend on the proportional use of fats and carbohydrates taking into account the severity and duration of the activity to be performed, general diet and degree of general fitness. Fats are more efficient than carbohydrates in that one gramme of fat produces about nine calories of heat to four calories from one gramme of carbohydrates. Fats become essential only when it is necessary to supply very large amounts of energy for prolonged physical work. The manipulation of fats and carbohydrates is regarded as a potential aid to enhancing performance.

Glycogen Diets can be modified to alter the amount of glycogen stored in the muscles and liver, particularly for those sportsmen and women whose events are of an endurance nature. Glycogen supercharging or glycogen supercompensation is most commonly practised by marathon runners. Briefly, it involves the athlete depleting his or her stores of glycogen with an intensive work-out about one week prior to a major competition. The athlete then follows a three-day diet consisting mainly of fats and proteins. Three to four days before the competition, the athlete indulges in large intakes of only carbohydrates in the hope of boosting and recharging the muscle glycogen stores, enabling him or her to endure physical activity for a longer period.

Vitamins Vitamin supplementation has also been a practice among sportspeople as a means of enhancing their performance. Vitamins are undoubtedly a vital component of an individual's nutritional needs for the maintenance of good health. They are only required in very small amounts for such maintenance, and their effects on physical performance, when vitamin supplements are taken, is only marginal, since the research evidence does not reveal that any significant increase in performance exists.

Food intake The view that excessive intakes of food increase an individual's bulk or body weight depends on several factors. A person's body composition will alter if a large and regular diet is maintained without any form of physical activity. With such a life-style that person may become obese. Conversely, excessive activity with too small a diet will likewise alter a person's body composition and will hinder performance. That person will possibly become very thin. To avoid the extremes of obesity and thinness, a balance between diet and activity must be found.

Physique An individual's physique depends primarily upon physiological make-up, metabolic rate, the quantity and type of food ingested, the type and severity of activity, the regularity of activity and the conditions under which it is performed. Other factors which must be considered are an individual's adaptability, acquaintance with and efficiency to perform physical exercises, age, and the sex of the individual. In the light of the factors mentioned, it should be clear that diet and the exercise schedule will affect an individual's physique and performance differently, since everyone responds and adapts uniquely to the wide range of foodstuffs available. Diets and training schedules should, therefore, be tailored to individuals separately and not, as often happens, to a group of people. To copy identically a champion's training programme and diet will not necessarily make a champion. Life is far more flexible than that, due to the many differences, mental and physical, among every individual.

2 Fatigue – its causes and effects on performance

Fatigue is an elusive concept presenting certain difficulties in its definition, measurement and interpretation. The term encompasses many facets and its causes are numerous and varied. It may be due to many hours of work, working environment, ventilation and type of employment. Broadly, fatigue symptoms may be caused by physiological and psychological factors. Fatigue may be acute, as caused by hard physical activity, or chronic. The latter is cumulative in its effects and is seldom relieved by rest or sleep as acute fatigue would be. Chronic fatigue is essentially of a psychological or psychiatric origin, characterized by lassitude, boredom, poor motivation, staleness or anxiety. Many sportsmen and women and weight trainers show such signs, hence the importance of variation in training and motivation. It is frequently considered that fatigue symptoms are present whenever a decrease in activity exists. Fatigue may, however, develop because of the effects of drugs, illness or lack of motivation, thus reducing the physical capacity to work. These factors, in fact, can cause fatigue even if no work is done.

Physiological and psychological aspects

The study of fatigue has involved physiological and psychological aspects since it is caused by certain physical and mental phenomena. The physiological aspect involves the study of the neuromuscular mechanisms and chemical reactions within the body as a consequence of exercise. The psychological aspect concerns the mental processes and the subjective feelings associated with fatigue. These would include discomfort, exhaustion, stress and anxiety. Difficulty arises, however, in dividing the causes of fatigue into the physiological and psychological categories, since fatigue may be the result of one single factor or could be caused by a combination of factors.

Fatigue in muscular performance will depend on an individual's willingness to perform a given task or exercise and the extent of his or her sensitivity and tolerance to pain. The onset of fatigue may also be caused by habituation, which means a decrease in response resulting from repetition. A sportsman or woman's work capacity may also be reduced owing to his or her loss of body fluids, such as heat loss through sweating during prolonged exercise.

If exercise is continued without any fluid replacement, dehydration will ensue.

It must be appreciated that fatigue, a term often used loosely, is caused by a multitude of factors. Basically, it refers to a deterioration of an activity or task as a direct result of being engaged in it. Fatigue may become apparent due to a single cause or a combination of several factors. Due to the diverse factors which can cause fatigue symptoms, the terms will always evade precise definition.

3 Ergogenic aids

The increase of muscular performance has always been the endeavour of man but in particular of sports participants, industrialists and the military. Industrialists have looked for new ways of increasing productivity with the most efficient use of human effort. The military have always been concerned with how servicemen can function most effectively under hostile conditions. But perhaps the group which has attracted the greatest publicity for methods of improving human performance has been that of the sports participant.

A variety of ways have been developed to improve human performance and new methods are always being sought. Basically, anything which is considered to elevate performance beyond normal expectations comes under the broad term *ergogenic aids*. The vast range of ergogenic aids may be broadly classified into two categories, substances and certain phenomena. The latter would include such phenomena as warm-up, information feedback, music, mental rehearsal, hypnosis and hot and cold applications. Such phenomena have been known to help certain sports participants to improve their performances and their use is considered to have no immoral or unethical implications.

The types of *substances* used as ergogenic aids are manifold, but include drugs, hormone manipulations and dietary supplements. Drugs form a small portion of the aids available to enhance human performance, and may be regarded as any substance which alters the metabolic and chemical composition of the body.

Drug usage　Sportsmen and sportswomen, particularly athletes, appear to have an insatiable appetite to produce new landmarks in sporting performances. Unfortunately, some are willing to resort to any method to achieve phenomenal records despite the possible consequences of long term drug ingestion. Drugs used in sport have been on the international scene for the past two decades, and their use continues to be widespread and on the increase, despite the attempts of certain governing bodies to eliminate such practices.

People are taking certain drugs at a very early age wishing for early success. Drugs have been used by participants in a variety of sports. Certain clinical implications are inherent with the habitual drug taker, the damage often being irreversible. We, the authors, condemn the use of drugs solely with the intent and purpose of improving sporting performances. Drugs should only be used for clinical benefit by those suffering from some physiological disorder or malfunction, and then under the strictest guidance of a physician.

Variety of drugs　Although we condemn the use of drugs in sport, we feel that it is important for coaches and aspiring sportsmen and sportswomen to make themselves conversant with the variety of drugs used in sport and their possible consequences in terms of damaged health. A host of drugs are available, such as caffeine, alkalis, adrenaline, alcohol, aspartates, amphetamines and steroids. Not all of these drugs have been studied sufficiently and scientifically to ascertain whether they do, in fact, improve human performance.

Many sportspeople have included the use of drugs as an integral part of their training schedule, and drugs which are considered to be dangerous, yet supposedly improve performance, do not deter some sports participants. Some drugs have become more popular among certain competitors primarily because their properties suggest that they should increase physical work and research studies have shown evidence to this effect.

Dosage　Physicians have always been confronted with a problem when prescribing a drug and that is dosage. It is commonly held that there are individual differences in response to specific drugs and dosages. Some people show an apparent and regular response to a given drug whilst others may show very little or no response, in spite of having taken the same dosage. Such differences may be due to the recipients' mental states and their physiological receptivity to certain drugs.

Everyone is unique in terms of personality, mental stability and general well-being. Such factors have important influences on the response to a drug. Long term or habitual users of a particular drug may eventually depress or reduce the physiological receptivity of that drug, so that the individual becomes tolerant to it. The symptoms may re-emerge because the effectiveness of the drug is less, due to the individual's increased tolerance to the drug. Therefore, to ward off such symptoms a greater dosage is required.

The diversity of drugs used by sports participants, whether taken orally or intra-muscularly, is beyond the imagination. There has been much public concern over the vast range of drugs used by sports participants because drug taking does have certain sociological, medical and ethical implications. It is difficult to ascertain which are the most prominent drugs used for the sole purpose of improving human performance. Amphetamines and anabolic steroids have perhaps been the most widely documented.

Amphetamines   A great variety of drugs are classified as amphetamines. They are used by sports participants whose event or sport is of an endurance nature. They have a pronounced effect on the function of the sympathetic nervous system, hence they are sometimes referred to as *sympathomimetic* drugs. Amphetamines are powerful stimulants causing increased alertness, increase in heart rate and blood pressure. Their greatest action is, however, to suppress or abolish the subjective symptoms of fatigue but fatigue, although a hindrance to performance, is an expected consequence of physical exertion. The various subjective feelings of fatigue serves as a warning system to the sportsperson to abandon completely or reduce energy output. The action of amphetamines dims or masks this warning sign, thus permitting the sportsperson to continue effort beyond normal expectations. However, when the effects of the drug wane or wear off, fatal consequences may result.

Another serious consequence of amphetamine ingestion is the onset of anorexia or loss of appetite.

Anabolic steroids   Anabolic steroids have supposedly been used by many athletes in a variety of events. Several leading world athletes have been found to have taken steroids. Although a life ban has been imposed on such athletes they can, in fact, re-emerge on the international scene. Legislation to ban athletes proven to have taken steroids is still not clearly established and international rules must be made for all the governing sporting bodies to agree and adhere to if some form of control of drug abuse in sport is to be achieved.

Anabolic steroids resemble the male sex hormone, both chemically and functionally. Steroids are physiologically potent and have many undesirable side effects, most notably liver impairment. In spite of the dangerous consequences of steroid ingestion, many young athletes may be tempted to take steroids in the hope of improving their performance. If steroids are taken before puberty, a decrease in height or stunted growth may result due to the cessation of growth of all the long bones in the body. Such consequences may cause certain psychological problems to the individual in later life. On all accounts, anabolic steroids should only be used for clinical purposes.

Research findings Evidence from research into the effects of anabolic steroids on body weight, muscular strength, and muscle size is conflicting and inconclusive. Many reasons may be cited for the cause of contrasting results by different researchers, including the variations in their methodology or procedural manner of conducting experiments, sample size, statistical analysis, type of steroid used, past experience of subjects and their psychological make-up, and the conditions under which the investigation is conducted. Several researchers have found that an increase in body weight occurs when steroids are taken, due possibly to water retention and fat accumulation rather than lean muscle mass. Other researchers have found no significant weight gain, gain in muscle mass or in strength, in spite of conducting their investigation on similar lines to those researchers finding significant changes in these dimensions. The effect of anabolic steroids on human performance and certain growth dimensions remains inconclusive.

Conclusion The only obvious conclusion one can draw, however, as with all drug abuse, is that greater control is needed by all governing bodies over the availability of such drugs, and a more positive action taken against offenders. The side-effects of anabolic steroids are numerous and serious and the damage is usually irreversible. The cliche 'prevention is better than cure' is most apt in the case of drug abuse. The topic of drugs in sport has become very important in recent years and it is impossible to give a full review in this book, but it is hoped that a broad outline has been given, and above all that the message has come across clearly. Remember, an increased performance does not necessarily mean improved health.

4 Sports injuries

The problem of sports injuries or sports medicine has long been a neglected one. Gradually, more efforts are being made to alleviate it and clinics are being set up, but a far greater scope is still necessary to meet the vast demand of sportsmen and women whose injuries are becoming more frequent. The frequency of sports injuries may be due to increased participation, greater aggression in contact games, greater intensity of training, more frequent competitions and recurrent injuries due to lack of recovery time, incorrect diagnosis, incorrect treatment or resuming competition too soon. Many types of sports injuries are peculiar to certain activities while others may be common to all sports and not solely caused by active sport participation, such as fractures and bruises. Nevertheless, injuries caused by involvement in sport usually present certain difficulties in terms of diagnosis and treatment.

Faulty or poor technique

There are various causes for sports injuries. Perhaps most notable is that of faulty or poor technique. Sports participants whose sport or event is regarded as technical in terms of execution, continually need the watchful guidance of a coach throughout their sporting careers. Poor technique often results in unnecessary strain and effort in various parts of the body, which will lead to discomfort and problems after frequent repetition. The whole purpose of acquiring good technique is to economize effort to concentrate all energies on the mechanical efficiency of the body, which will result in better performances. This is very true of the weight trainer or lifter, hence the importance of correct lifting techniques.

Clothing and footwear

Another major cause of injuries to sports participants and which often gets overlooked is clothing and footwear. Too loose or tight fitting clothes and improper footwear, or badly worn shoes, can cause injury by tripping or slipping. Ill fitting clothes can impede movement and get caught in the apparatus being used. Therefore, it is important to ensure that good protective and correctly fitting sports gear is worn during sporting activities.

Contact sports

Many sports injuries are inevitable, especially in contact sports. Rules governing a particular sport will reduce the chances or severity of injuries if these rules are correctly implemented and the referee controls the game strictly. Perhaps the ruling of some sporting bodies requires modification to diminish the likelihood of accidents during injury-prone sports.

Reaction to injury

Sportsmen and women generally react to injuries or illnesses differently to the non-sporting person. If the injury or condition is regarded as trivial, then the sportsperson may ignore it and continue to train and perhaps compete, in the hope of 'running it off'. Unfortunately, the injury may recur with the consequence of bringing training and competition to a grinding halt. In some cases a minor injury does heal with continued but modified training. Frequently, however, the injury is exacerbated, but to what extent will depend on the nature and cause of the injury as well as the type of training performed. The important point to note is that medical advice should be sought as soon as possible, however minor the injury may be. Meanwhile, a sensible and modified approach to training can be performed whilst awaiting medical advice.

Variety of injuries

The variety of injuries incurred during sporting activities is extremely vast. The extent of an injury may range from very mild to very severe and it is impossible to cover the entire scope adequately in this book. The important point, however, is to be aware of the possible complications if an injury is neglected, and of the importance of seeking medical advice as a preventative measure, to avoid regrets at a later date.

People who are recommended to return to work by their general practitioner following an injury or illness should not necessarily resume their training. A sportsman or sportswoman must make the exact nature of his or her sport clear to whoever is treating him or her, and that he or she wishes to resume training as soon as possible. If this information is witheld, then the sportsperson is not going to get the maximum benefit from the various forms of treatment available. The only recommendation he or she is likely to receive is 'complete rest'. This is often frustrating for the energetic and active sportsperson.

Physical activity

The experience of all sports participants is that maintenance of 'physical fitness' depends mostly on physical activity. It takes several years to reach a high standard of physical performance but the level of fitness drops very rapidly if training is discontinued. It is obvious that, to maintain general good health and fitness, exercising must be a life-long process. Absence for too long from activity or exercises soon causes a deterioration of physical capacity and it takes a long time to regain the same level of fitness.

Muscle wastage

Too frequently, the slightest injury or illness is a good enough excuse for many people to forego exercise or miss work. A complete break from exercising can only be justified if an injury is very serious but the unaffected areas of the body can still be given specific exercises to maintain good muscle tone and the well-being of the individual. It is inevitable that deterioration in muscle strength and bulk will occur in the immediate areas of the injury or injuries. However, with special guidance from a remedial gymnast or physiotherapist, specific exercises can be performed to delay muscle wastage and loss of function.

The section on muscles (see pages 2–7) explained that the function of skeletal muscles is contraction. If muscles are not contracted or used, they will atrophy or waste away. Therefore, some form of activity must be maintained during the recovery period after an injury or illness. This may seem harsh but generally in life one has to be cruel to be kind. If no exercises are performed during the healing of an injury, the general state and well-being of the patient becomes much worse and other problems emerge in addition to the original injury. It is therefore important that some form of active treatment be prescribed by those qualified to give guidance and supervision, for example, remedial gymnasts and physiotherapists.

The section on types of muscle contraction and the group action of muscles explained the importance of muscle contraction from a rehabilitation point of view. Exercises to aid recovery from sports injuries should be performed gradually and progressively, under control.

Inform the coach It is important that sports participants keep their coach or adviser informed of their injury, the treatment they are receiving and the progress being made. After all, the coach plays an integral part in the sports participants' training and competitive schedule and this should also include management and awareness of sports injuries.

A sportsman or woman who has recently recovered from an injury and has regained full fitness should continue to consult his or her medical adviser at regular intervals to ensure that complete healing has in fact occurred.

General outline In the space available, we have only been able to give a general outline of sports injuries, for the diversity of both causes and types of injury prevalent in sport today is enormous, and a separate specialist section on medicine would be needed. Each injury has to be treated as a separate case, although it may be the same and be caused in the same manner as in another person. People's responses to an injury and its treatment differ. The sportsperson must seek medical advice soon after an injury has been incurred to prevent further complications developing, but admittedly this is often difficult to do. Above all, he or she must be patient and not become too eager to train too severely before a full recovery has been made.

5 Psychological aspects of training and competition

Numerous physiological and psychological factors contribute to the limitation of human performance. Improved training methods and more knowledgeable coaching have permitted sportsmen and sportswomen to develop their optimum potential in terms of strength and cardiorespiratory efficiency, but having acquired peak fitness and optimum skill levels, a sportsperson striving for further improvement in competition or training must rely on psychological factors such as motivation and arousal.

Fatigue, which has already been discussed (see page 121), is obviously a factor affecting performance, regardless of the level of skill acquired. The various symptoms associated with fatigue, whether physiological or psychological, are important in that they act as warning devices to prevent over-exertion and perhaps fatal consequences.

Pain, a normal consequence of severe exertion, usually ensures the long term safety of the body by protecting it from injury by slowing or halting physical activity.

Motivation and arousal

The concept of motivation encompasses many facets but it is sufficient for our purposes to regard it as the level of desire to excel and succeed. Motivation is closely related to the concept of drive or arousal, and it has been accepted that a relationship exists between levels of performance and arousal. Recognition of this was as early as 1908 when Yerkes and Dodson found in a study of rats that as levels of motivation were increased for a given task an optimum level of performance was reached, but further increases in motivation produced a deterioration in performance. This is often referred to as the *inverted 'u' hypothesis* and is depicted in figure 62. Such a relationship has been linked to human performance, and suggests that a certain level of motivation or arousal is necessary if an improvement in efficiency and performance is to be attained. However, increased levels of arousal, such as high excitement, would produce a gradual decrease in performance. Frequently sportspeople, when they have performed below their usual form, say 'I tried too hard', and it follows, therefore, that some point in the middle range of arousal is most suitable for optimal performance.

There are numerous means by which motivation or arousal may be increased, such as intrinsic motivation for personal interest and desires, financial rewards, the competition itself, the presence of spectators, honour, the will to win and so on.

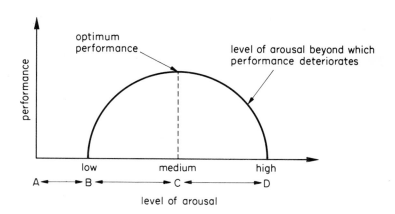

Figure 62 Inverted 'u' hypothesis

A – B = subthreshold level of arousal, for example, deep sleep or coma

B – C = submaximal levels of arousal

C = optimum performance or maximum level of arousal

C – D = excess levels of arousal

Task difficulty

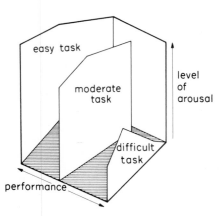

(adapted from P L Broadhurst, 1957)

Figure 63 Relationship between arousal and increasing task difficulty

Optimum level of performance.

The level of arousal may also be affected by the difficulty of the task being performed. It is apparent that some sports are more difficult to execute than others and this also applies to the vast variety of weight training exercises. It is thought that complex or difficult tasks are best performed when an individual's arousal or motivation is relatively low but optimum proficiency in what may be regarded as a simple task is best attained when the arousal is high. This is illustrated diagrammatically in figure 63 which is an adaptation of Broadhurst's (1957) model using three levels of difficulty. It can be deduced from this model that optimum arousal for learning and performing physical tasks is decreased with increasing task difficulty.

It can be seen from figures 62 and 63 that the main factors involved in performance lie in the level of motivation or arousal, and in the difficulty of the task. A sportsperson must endeavour to strive for optimal performance to succeed, reaching, ideally, the highest peak of the curve. Lack or loss of motivation will fail to produce optimal performance, whereas levels too high will result in a decrease in performance.

The optimum level of performance in a given task will generally depend upon several factors such as the nature of the task – whether difficult or easy – previous training, level of skill acquired, habits formed, and an individual's level of arousal. The arousal level of an athlete is generally near optimal since he or she is motivated but in highly competitive situations over-arousal can occur. This may be because many sporting activities involve onlookers, and the crowd has certain expectations of the athletes. Professional sportspeople may feel that there is extra pressure on them in the form of monetary rewards or responsibility for carrying national prestige in international competition. Such factors may motivate the athlete towards optimal performance, or over-arouse the athlete so that performance deteriorates. A drop in performance may occur in endurance events, or those which are highly repetitious, such as the high jump or pole vault, as the athlete begins to feel tired or bored. These two phenomena, tiredness and boredom due to high repetition, may be referred to as physiological and psychological fatigue respectively. Once either of these occur, the athlete's level of arousal falls, resulting in a loss of performance, as depicted in the left portion of the inverted 'u' in figure 62. A deviation in either direction from the optimal level of arousal may be the difference between success and failure in top-level sport.

Personality   An athlete's optimum arousal for performance is affected by his or her personality. The concept of personality encompasses many facets present in an individual's psychological make-up. Several theories have been postulated but here Eysenck's theory of personality will be discussed.

Eysenck regards personality as permanent and consistent patterns of behaviour and uses the terms *introversion* and *extraversion* as extremes of behaviour. Extremes of these personality types rarely exist among people. Many lie between the two. Extraverts in Eysenck's view are outgoing, relatively uninhibited, aggressive, cravers for excitement, unreliable, optimistic and easy going. Introverts tend to possess the opposite of these qualities. Eysenck contends that introverts have a relatively high level of arousal, compared to extraverts. Extraverts are considered to suffer from 'stimulus hunger', which accounts for their being generally fond of noise, alcohol, and sociability in their search for further stimuli. The introvert is less susceptible to stimulation, and may even find the environment too stimulating, and therefore he or she seeks peace and quiet.

Relating this to the inverted 'u' performance curve, introverts tend to begin at a higher level of arousal than extraverts. Introverts and extraverts will react differently to competition and the presence of spectators. Introverts may become over-aroused compared to extraverts since they are already highly aroused.

Athletes often have problems in performing at their optimum in major competitions. Some frequently perform well in training and at minor meetings but not so well in important competitions. Analysis of the athlete's personality in terms of Eysenck's introversion and extraversion theory may help to explain this strange phenomenon.

Appendix

Conversion table

kilos	lb	kilos	lb	kilos	lb	kilos	lb
25	55	137½	303	250	551	362½	799
27½	61	140	308½	252½	556½	365	804½
30	66	142½	314	255	562	367½	810
32½	72	145	319½	257½	567½	370	815½
35	77	147½	325	260	573	372½	821
37½	83	150	330½	262½	578½	375	826½
40	88	152½	336	265	584	377½	832
42½	94	155	341½	267½	589½	380	837¾
45	99	157½	347	270	595	382½	843¼
47½	104½	160	352½	272½	600¾	385	848¾
50	110	162½	358	275	606¼	387½	854¼
52½	115½	165	363¾	277½	611¼	390	859¾
55	121¼	167½	369¼	280	617¼	392½	865¼
57½	126¾	171	374¾	282½	622¾	395	870¾
60	132¼	172½	380¼	285	628¼	397½	876¼
62½	137¾	175	385¾	287½	633¾	400	881¾
65	143¼	177½	391¼	290	639¼	402½	887¼
67½	148¾	180	396¾	292½	644¾	405	892¾
70	154¼	182½	402¼	295	650¼	407½	898¼
72½	159¾	185	407¾	297½	655¾	410	903¾
75	165¼	187½	413¼	300	661¼	412½	909¼
77½	170¾	190	418¾	302½	666¾	415	914¾
80	176½	192½	424¼	305	672¼	417½	920¼
82½	181¾	195	429¾	307¼	677¾	420	925¾
85	187¼	197½	435¼	310	683¼	422½	931¼
87½	192¾	200	440¾	312½	688¾	425	936¾
90	198¼	202½	446¼	315	694¼	427½	942¼
92½	203¾	205	451¾	317½	699¾	430	947¾
95	209¼	207½	457¼	320	705¼	432½	953¼
97½	214¾	210	462¾	322½	710¾	435	959
100	220¼	212½	468¼	325	716½	437½	964½
102½	225¾	215	473¾	327½	722	440	970
105	231¼	217½	479½	330	727½	442½	975½
107½	236¾	220	485	332½	733	445	981
110	241½	222½	490½	335	738½	447½	986½
112½	248	225	496	337½	744	450	992
115	253½	227½	501½	340	749½	452½	997½
117½	259	230	507	342½	755	455	1003
120	264½	232½	512½	345	760½	457½	1008½
122½	270	235	518	347½	766	460	1014
125	275½	237½	523½	350	771½	462½	1019½
127½	281	240	529	352½	777	465	1025
130	286½	242½	534½	355	782½	467½	1030½
132½	292	245	540	357½	788	470	1036
135	297½	247½	545½	360	793½		

Bibliography

BURKE, E. J. (1980) *Toward an Understanding of Human Performance*, 2nd edition. New York: Movement Publications.

DELORME, T. L. and WATKINS, A. L. (1951) *Progressive Resistance Exercise*. New York: Appleton-Century-Crofts.

DE VRIES, H. A. (1966) *Physiology of Exercise for Physical Education and Athletics*. Dubuque, Iowa: Wm C. Brown.

EYSENCK, H. J. (1967) *The Biological Basis of Personality*. Springfield, Ill.: Charles C. Thomas.

HOFFMAN, B. (1961) *Weight Training for Athletes*. New York: Ronald Press.

KARPOVITCH, P. V. (1971) *Physiology of Muscular Activity*, 7th edition. Philadelphia, Pa.: W. B. Saunders.

LEAR, J. (1980) *Weight Training*. East Ardsley, Wakefield: E. P. Publishing.

MOREHOUSE, L. E. and MILLER, A. T. (1971) *Physiology of Exercise*, 6th edition. St Louis, Mo.: The C. V. Mosby Co.

O'SHEA, J. P. (1966) *Scientific Principles and Methods of Strength Fitness*. Corvallis, Or.: Oregon State University Book Stores.

WELLS, K. F. (1971) *Kinesiology*, 5th edition. Philadelphia, Pa.: W. B. Saunders.

Articles and papers

BROADHURST, P. L. (1957) 'Emotionality and the Yerkes-Dodson Law'. *Journal of Experimental Psychology,* 54: 345–52.

PIPES, T. V. and WILMORE, J. H. (1975) 'Isokinetic versus isotonic strength training in adult men'. *Medicine and Science in Sport*, 7: 262–74.

PIPES, T. V. and WILMORE, J. H. (1976) 'Muscular strength through isotonic and isokinetic resistance training'. *Athletic Journal*, 57: 42–5.

YERKES, R. M. and DODSON, J. D. (1908) 'The relation of strength of stimulus to rapidity of habit formation'. *Journal of Comparative Neurological Psychology*, 18: 459–82.

Index